Jackie French is an award-w
negotiator and the Australi
for 2014–2015. She is regarded as one of Australia's
most popular children's authors, and writes across
all genres — from picture books, history, fantasy,
ecology and sci-fi to her much loved historical fiction.
In her capacity as Australian Children's Laureate,
'Share a Story' will be the primary philosophy behind
Jackie's two-year term.

You can visit Jackie's website at
www.jackiefrench.com

I SPY A

GREAT READER

HOW TO UNLOCK THE LITERACY SECRET AND GET YOUR CHILD HOOKED ON BOOKS

JACKIE FRENCH

THE AUSTRALIAN CHILDREN'S LAUREATE

Angus&Robertson
An imprint of HarperCollins*Publishers*

Angus & Robertson
An imprint of HarperCollins*Publishers*
First published in Australia in 2014
by HarperCollins*Publishers* Australia Pty Limited
ABN 36 009 913 517
harpercollins.com.au

HarperCollins*Publishers*
Level 13, 201 Elizabeth Street, Sydney NSW 2000, Australia
Unit D1, 63 Apollo Drive, Rosedale, Auckland 0632, New Zealand
A 53, Sector 57, Noida, UP, India
1 London Bridge Street, London, SE1 9GF, United Kingdom
2 Bloor Street East, 20th floor, Toronto, Ontario M4W 1A8, Canada
195 Broadway, New York NY 10007, USA

National Library of Australia Cataloguing-in-Publication data:

French, Jackie, author.
 I spy a great reader: unlock the literary secret and get your child hooked on
 books / Jackie French.
 978 0 7322 9952 1 (paperback)
 978 1 4607 0340 3 (ebook)
 Reading – Parent participation
 Children – Books and reading.
 Reading readiness.
649.58

Cover design by Christa Moffitt, Christabella Designs
Cover images: Children reading story by Ross Anania/ Getty Images;
background images by shutterstock.com
Back cover photograph of Jackie French © Kelly Sturgiss

CONTENTS

Introduction   1

Chapter 1   Reading to your baby   9
What reading to a baby will give them   10
What you gain from reading to a baby   11
How to read to a baby   13
When to read to your baby   15
Babies' book clubs and libraries   16
Other ways to help your baby develop into a reader
    (and all-round clever kid)   16
Milestones   20

Chapter 2   Two to three years   21
Don't push kids to learn!   22
Let kids choose the books — most of the time   22
How to read to two- to three-year-olds   23
Which books to read?   24
Reading games for two- to three-year-olds   28
Learning whole words   31
Reading projects for two- to three-year-olds   35
Games for two- to three-year-olds   36
Work out how your child likes to learn   42

Chapter 3   Three to five years   44
How to read to three- to five-year-olds   45
Reading, not writing   46
How to tell if a child is ready to learn to read   47
How to teach a child to read   48
Reading games for three- to five-year-olds   49
How to find lots of books
    without breaking the bank   57
When to ask for help   58
You don't have to do it all   61

Chapter 4   How to teach basic reading   63
When to teach a child to read   64
Three steps to reading   65
How to learn sounds   66
Don't try to do it all   76
Learning the hard words   77
How to teach and read at the same time   80
How to read sentences   83
Ways to help a child read a book   84
How to read bigger books   87
Find the magic book   88

Chapter 5   Helping with reading   90
The four Rs: Regular, Revise, Relax and Reward   90
A step-by-step guide   91
You can't read if you don't have a book   93
Entrancing 'learn to read' books for all ages   94

Chapter 6   Handwriting and spelling   100
Helping with handwriting   100
How to help with spelling   103

Chapter 7   Homework, essays and stories   108
How to write an essay (a beginner's guide)   108
How to write stories   111
What kids get from writing stories   113
Creating a story step by step   114
How to make your stories better   119
Some issues people have with writing   126
How to get kids to love writing stories   131
Helping with homework   138

**Chapter 8   Reading problems and teaching
            problems: and how to help**   142
How to tell if kids have learning problems   143
The first great dyslexia myth   145
The second great dyslexia myth   146
Other dyslexia myths debunked   146

Kids who learn differently   147
Visual learners   149
Verbal, auditory or sound learners   151
Fast processors   154
Social learners   158
Active children and kinetic learners   160
Kinetic learners   162
Easily distracted children   166
Slow learners   171
Slow language developers   173
Bright but bored children   176
Children who have just missed out   179
Physical problems that interfere with reading:
    and how to help   180
Visual problems   184
Hearing problems   188
Attention disorders   192
Coordination problems   196
Eating problems   199
Lack of sleep   201
Pain   202
Family issues, stress and worries   203
Help from a Psychologist or Psychiatrist   205
Noise and disruption at home   206
Stress at school   208
Seeking professional tutoring   210

Chapter 9   Teenagers   215
Teenagers who can't read   216
Finding time   218
How to help teenagers who have missed out   220
How to help teenagers get books   226
Helping teenagers with spelling   227

Chapter 10   Getting kids hooked on books   229
Why it's important to give kids the books they love   232
How to make kids bored with reading   232
How to help kids find the books they love   234

Other people's magic books   240
Why a good book will always be more vivid than TV   243
Non-fiction magic   244

Chapter 11   Family reading   **249**
What and when to read together   251
The books kids shouldn't have   257
A quick guide to what to read when   265

Chapter 12   Book groups for everyone   **267**
Book groups for littlies (3 months to school age)   267
Reading groups for early readers   269
Primary school reading groups   269
Teenage book club   271

Chapter 13   A classroom revolution   **273**
How we fail our kids   274
No kid is hopeless   279
What our schools could be like   282
The microphone solution   282
Outdoor classrooms   283
Add movement   284
Let kids talk in class   286
Make school theirs   287
Encourage projects   292
Teach that teachers are human   293
Lovable libraries for kids   294
It's only paper: encouraging kids to read when
    they eat (the art of reading with sticky fingers)   298

Appendix
How volunteers can help: the evolution of a volunteer
    tutoring group — Youth Educational Support
    Service (YESS)   301

INTRODUCTION

Every child *can* learn to read.

Every child *must* learn to read.

Reading makes kids more intelligent. It doesn't just make them seem more intelligent: reading creates new neural connections in a child's brain by stimulating the growth of new neurons as they imagine the world the writer has put on paper.

TV, movies and electronic games don't do this — they spoon-feed their worlds to a child. But every universe a child reads about is created by him or her in partnership with the writer.

If you want your kids to be more intelligent, give them books.

If you want them to learn empathy, to understand how others feel, give them books, because stories give kids this too.

Every book they read shows children how others feel or see the world. Nothing — nothing! — can equal this.

Reading is the most vital skill we learn at school.

Reading doesn't just give you knowledge. It gives you the tools to use knowledge. Once there were many jobs that meant you could get by without knowing how to read. These days online material is a vital part of modern social and administrative life. A child who can't read is deeply excluded from our society.

And reading means you are part of the world of books. A book is a small, transportable, delightful universe you can keep in your handbag, glovebox or desk drawer, and take out to vanish into when the world is not as you would like it to be.

But about one in ten Australian kids can't read well enough to work their way through a simple book suited to their age. Worse: few of them get professional help. How could we let this happen?

There are many reasons a child may not learn to read, but there are no excuses. None.

Some kids fall behind in their first year of school, sometimes because they have a problem with hearing how words sound or with visually tracking them on the page. Other kids may need to be taught in different ways: outdoors rather than in the classroom, or where they can talk about what they learn with their friends.

Often the problem isn't noticed in the first or even second year at school. Dyslexic kids are often very bright indeed. She'll ask her best friend what the book says or he'll find other ways to cover up his embarrassment. But the longer the problem is ignored or unnoticed, the more they have to catch up.

All too often, the problem *is* picked up, but shrugged off. 'Kids learn at different rates,' a parent will be told. 'Don't worry, they'll catch up.' And indeed some do — but many don't. And they won't — not unless someone steps in to help.

Even today, many teachers assume that kids with problems *can't* be taught. Last year I sat in a school staffroom while the teachers of kids I was about to work with made comments such as, 'They're hopeless. I don't know why we bother.' Every kid I met in this 'hopeless' group was intelligent and perceptive. They were not failures — the *school* had failed *them* — but they were convinced that they were stupid. It is so very, very easy to convince a child he or she is dumb. Once this happens the scars never truly fade.

It would be good to think that all kids will be taught to read by well-trained and committed professionals.

Every school needs a literacy teacher who can refer kids to specialists if they have a problem with tracking words on the page or in hearing distinct syllables, and who will work out the best way for that student to learn.

Every school needs to accept that if children can't read the material their peers are reading, they must have extra daily help until they can.

Every school needs teacher librarians who can guide kids to books they'll love so much they'll force themselves to read just to see what happens next.

Every teacher needs to accept that all kids can learn to read and write, and that if they haven't yet they need to be taught in different ways, including by using Braille or by touch-typing for kids whose brains can't see words as patterns.

Perhaps, one day, we'll reach that ideal. Until then, parents and volunteers need to know how to teach kids instead. Teachers who work in schools without a literacy specialist need to know how to help and support the kids who do have reading problems.

Because everyone *can* read. I'm dyslexic. I can't follow or even remember a city map; I get lost in car parks; can't see when a word is misspelt, nor read a form easily or follow if someone runs their finger under a line on the page. But I can read. Fast. I just don't read the way most kids are taught to. There are many, many ways to read.

Even if your child is going to sail through school with no problems, this book will help them grow into their full potential in the preschool years. The early years of a child's life are the most valuable of all in teaching both the skills that will become the basics of literacy and how to be fulfilled and open to happiness. This book will help to show the way.

MATTHEW'S STORY

Matthew was a bright kid. He learnt to walk and talk earlier than other kids. He could remember every item in My Grandmother's Trunk (page 37). But in his first year at school he just couldn't pick up reading.

Don't worry, said his teacher. Kids learn at different rates. He's just a bit slower. That's what they said in his second and third year at school too.

In his fourth year, the school admitted there was a problem. He received one hour a week with a reading recovery teacher. It didn't help his reading. It even made the problem worse, because Matthew saw kids who he knew weren't as bright as him learning to read, and he couldn't even manage to decode the few basic words on the page. All that one hour a week taught him was that he was dumb.

Matthew was given more help by untrained volunteer parents. He was pretty sure, he told me years afterwards, that back home they were laughing: 'That kid Matthew is ten years old, and he can't read yet.'

Matthew was lucky. He changed schools when he was twelve. This new school sent him to an educational psychologist. The psychologist diagnosed a major learning problem. Matthew was in the 99.7th percentile of intelligence, but still couldn't read *The cat sat on the mat*'. He was given a laptop computer, and coordination and tracking exercises. Within three months he had taught himself to read and write. It took another year to catch up on all the literacy lessons he had missed.

But he *still* thought he was dumb. He assumed he'd fail the year twelve exams — somehow the school had been fooled into thinking he was bright, but now everyone would know how stupid he really was. He did brilliantly. But at his first university exams he panicked again — surely now the world would see that he was stupid. Once again he sailed through them. I don't know where he is now, but I suspect he is still doing brilliantly — and still, deep down, those voices from his childhood are still whispering, 'Hey kid. You're dumb.'

Another school failed to notice a child's inability to track words along a line, so that at ten she still couldn't read. She picked up the basics of writing in one afternoon when the problem was finally diagnosed. A six-year-old boy was diagnosed with Attention Deficit Disorder, but within four months of work with an occupational therapist he had learnt how to concentrate. Like Matthew, he is now doing brilliantly too. So often kids with learning problems — or who just need to learn differently — are brighter than average, often enormously so.

> *Every kid can read. It is the duty of everyone to provide a world where they can learn, and find the books they need.*

Other kids — perhaps 30–40 per cent — can read, but by ten years old they have decided that books are boring.

We've failed these kids, too.

There is a 'magic book' that will turn every kid into a reader. We just need to help them find it.

CHAPTER 1

READING TO YOUR BABY

The first time you read to a baby is one of the most magic moments in your life. Not only do you get to cuddle this beautiful, baby-scented small bundle, you are also sharing something essentially human: the power of words and the power of stories.

Babies can't talk, but they understand when you speak to them. They may not know most of the words in a book, though they may comprehend much more than you realise. But babies understand the *feel* of a story, just as they understand when you smile and say, 'Hello, Amelia!' in the morning.

What reading to a baby will give them

- The ability to concentrate. It takes at least five minutes to read a picture book to a baby. That's a long time for a baby to focus. But if they love the book — and love you reading to them — they'll concentrate till you finish, or even while you read it again and again.

- The concept of 'a story'. A story isn't true (mostly) it's 'just pretend'. 'Just pretend' is one of the most powerful human inventions. It's not a lie: it's what might be. Every invention, from the wheel to Einstein's Theory of Relativity, began with a version of 'let's pretend'. It's a sophisticated concept, but babies get it.

- What written words look like. By the time a baby is three months old they can distinguish the shapes of words and letters and lines on a page, and begin to remember what the most common ones look like. It took humans most of our history to invent the written word, as opposed to a drawing of or a symbol for something. If you read to your baby, he'll not just know what a word looks like, but begin to break it down into its component letters, to see the patterns. No, he isn't learning to read yet. But he is learning the skills of 'pre-reading', which will make reading far easier to learn. They may also read faster and learn new words more easily later on.

- How to track across a page. When we read English we track from left to right across the page, then back again to the left-hand side of the page but one line down. Like many dyslexics, I find that difficult.
- The whole 'book' concept: that books are made up of pages you turn to get to the next bit of the story. They have a beginning and an end, and exciting bits in the middle — and most books make sense only if you progress in a linear, directional fashion. Babies need to learn this too.
- That books are fun before you go to bed, when you just want to relax or when you are bored.

What you gain from reading to a baby

- Cuddles!
- Time out. Find the most comfy chair or sofa, get yourself a glass of something good, put your feet up, relax with baby in the crook of your arm or on your lap — and read.
- Fun. The best books for babies are fun for grown-ups too (at least till you have read them four hundred times).

Reading to a baby isn't just about the cuddle factor. If it was you could read a baby the telephone book, and she'd love it just as much as a picture book. Nor, sadly, will it ensure that your child grows up to be a genius. But it will give her a good start. Visualising creates new neurons and strengthens connections in the brain — mental muscle-building. The earlier you start the better the result.

But don't start with *War and Peace*, or even expect them to like every picture book. My five-month-old grandson Jack didn't like *Pete the Sheep* at all. (It's easy to see if a baby doesn't like a book. They kick it, cry, turn away or try to eat it — or all of the above. *Pete the Sheep*, is more fun for anyone over two years old, who laughs when you do the 'woof woof' and 'baa' sounds.)

Then I opened *Dinosaurs Love Cheese* — instant hit, partly for the bright colours, partly because there is a baby pictured on each page. Babies identify with babies. They like bright colours and wide smiles. They don't like big hats or hair that disguises those smiles. But they can also be distracted. There is a page in *Dinosaurs Love Cheese* where the tigers are camouflaged in the pizza parlour. Jack gave a cry of triumph when he first realised they were there, and waved his hands and crowed every time we came to that page again.

He understood the story too — or, rather, that it was a story, even if there was a lot he missed. Adults often assume that babies don't understand much of their speech because babies can't talk. You try talking with no teeth and a tongue you only started really working with a few months ago.

Babies lack vocabulary. Don't expect them to know what you mean by 'volcano' unless you live below one and it growls at lunchtime. But babies do understand the flow of words, and the differences between a conversation and a remark. And — by 12 months old, at least — understand that you are reading them a story, a tale connected to the marks on the page that you are pointing at.

When you first begin to read to your baby, he'll enjoy the cuddle and your voice more than the book. But by five months he will be well and truly able to enjoy the book for itself — as well as you reading it.

How to read to a baby

(Or: Bringing up a genius, Step 1)

- Choose a baby-friendly book: bright clear colours and, preferably, a baby and lots of smiles. They can be tiger smiles or human smiles, but the eyes should smile as well as the mouths. Kids identify with babies in a book, and very young babies judge people and animals by their smiles and expressions in their eyes. Go for lots of smiles and laughter.

- Read stories rather than ABC or counting books that are unrelated episodes. You want your child to understand the idea of 'book' and story, i.e.

consecutive text and ideas, one page leading to another. ABC and counting books can wait till they can make their own books.

- Be comfy, you and baby both, and sit where you can both see the book and it won't strain your wrist. Sitting on a sofa works when kids are old enough to snuggle next to you or on your lap. But with smaller kids try both of you lying on your tummy on a blanket on the floor, or baby lying and you with the book propped comfortably sitting beside them. N.B. if knees are creaky make sure there is a chair next to you so you can hoist yourself up.

- Let the babies choose their own books. They'll tell you if they're bored: mutter, yell, look away. But if they start beating their toes in rapt delight, you'll know this is the book for them. Most of the time, let *all* kids choose their own books. Yes, guide them, extend them but, if they are bored, let them read another book instead, just as we do as adults.

- Don't worry about sticky fingers and baby dribble. Babies are more precious than books. Even if it is your signed first edition, it will be better with a dribble mark too. In twenty years, or thirty or forty, you'll find that the dribble is more precious than the signature, as you remember the joy of reading, just you two, at the beginning of a life.

- Look for 'board books' made of laminated cardboard, so that babies can hold them and turn the pages more easily without creasing or tearing them. These books can also be wiped down if a bit of puréed carrot appears to decorate the pages.
- Read familiar books, so babies learn to recognise the words. Read new books to extend the words they recognise. A good balance is one 'old' book and one 'new' book each day. The new book stays new for about a week.

When to read to your baby

Establish routines: a story before bedtime, a story before naptimes.

But also read when either of you is hassled or bored. Keep a book in your bag to read in traffic jams, waiting in a queue at the supermarket, on a plane or waiting to board one. This is a great way to teach kids that you need never be bored when you can read a book (or daydream a story).

You'll find that once a baby has been read to for a few months and is old enough to hold a book, he will read to himself for a few minutes or even longer (if you are very lucky, up to half an hour). No, they are not reading, but they are remembering you reading to them. They may even be beginning to match the words they remember with the words on the page.

Babies' book clubs and libraries

Take your baby to the story time at the local library, or join (or form) a parents' group where you take it in turns to read a story each time to the kids. This teaches babies that all sorts of people read books, in all sorts of places.

Libraries are also great places to choose free books, and lots of different ones so you can vary what you read. But, if possible, do have at least half a dozen familiar books of your own. These don't just teach kids to recognise familiar words, they become loved companions when something unpleasant happens, like a visit to the doctor or teething.

Joining a babies' reading group also helps kids learn to play with each other. But their main advantage is for you: you get to talk to adults, hopefully have a good cup of coffee and a muffin, and exchange reassurances about what your baby is doing, and how to cope with lack of sleep, teething grumbles and grandparents with too much advice.

Other ways to help your baby develop into a reader (and all-round clever kid)

PLAY

Babyhood is the greatest learning time in a child's life. When you play with your baby you are beginning to teach her how to coordinate and concentrate.

Babies learn to concentrate on one thing for longer and longer periods of time. Play or talk to your baby until the point where he loses interest. Try to extend his concentration span at least once a day; he will slowly learn to concentrate for longer.

TALK

Talk to your child even before she can talk to you. Talk *lots.* Tell your child what you are doing and where you are going. 'Now Mummy is walking into the kitchen ...'; 'We're going to the shops ...'; 'Look at the apples in that bag over there'. For most children, the more they are exposed to words, the more words they'll pick up and the faster they'll learn to speak fluently.

Don't talk *all* the time, however. Give your child a chance to respond. Babies need to be given a chance to acknowledge what has been said — perhaps with a smile or a glance in the right direction or a sound, even if they can't talk yet.

If you want your child to learn as many words as possible so that he can express himself properly, you'll have to *talk* to him — and, of course, reading to him will increase his vocabulary.

HAVE CONVERSATIONS

Your baby is talking to you! Listen to the sounds a baby makes. It has a pattern, a bit like a song. It's prespeech. Your baby is joining in the conversation. Let her talk to you; listen and, if possible, don't interrupt.

TEACH BABIES WHAT WORDS SOUND LIKE

Speak as clearly and distinctly as you can, so that children learn what words *really* sound like. Speaking to children clearly makes it easier for them to learn to speak and understand language; it also makes it much simpler for them to understand that C-A-T spells *cat*, not just C then a grunt!

It's very difficult to learn to spell words if you don't know what they sound like. Think about a phrase like *thank you*. Mostly people say *than-ya* or *thang-yu*. A word like this would be easier to spell if it was pronounced clearly — and children need to learn that words are made up of different sounds put together.

When you are speaking to young children, speak as clearly as you can — not necessarily slowly, just clearly. Try to sound out the syllables in words — *chil-dren, thank you*. It doesn't matter if you don't do this all the time, but do it now and then so children learn what a word *should* sound like.

TURN OFF THE TV AND RADIO

Try to keep the TV or radio off as much as possible when kids are learning to speak, and especially when you read to them. It's *very* difficult for kids to distinguish individual sounds when there is lots of noise in the background. It's possible that many of the kids who have reading problems these days have never learnt to distinguish the sounds within words properly because a TV has always been on in the background.

TEACH COORDINATION: CRAWLING, DANCING AND CLAPPING

To read English you have to be able to make your eyes track from left to right, and move slowly down the page as you read down line after line. But some children — and adults like me — never learnt left from right. Children with coordination problems find it much more difficult to learn to read and write — how to start at the left-hand side of the page and follow the words across to the right-hand side. It sounds simple but, as I know all too well, it often isn't! Here are some ways to build coordination from the ground up.

- Encourage children to crawl — don't be in too much of a hurry to get them to walk. Crawling teaches left–right coordination.
- Play clapping games with them — their left hand on your left hand, their right hand on your right hand — while singing a song.
- Play hopping games, on one foot and then the other.
- Dance the Hokey-Pokey: 'Put your right foot in, put your right foot out, put your right foot in and you

shake it all about. You do the hokey-pokey and you turn around, and that's what it's all about!'

- These games are all bouncy fun, but what they teach is incredibly important. Children need at least one good bouncy coordination game every day.

Milestones

- By the time your baby is six months old she should be focusing on a picture book and following the story.
- By the time your baby is a year old he should be crawling and holding a book and turning the pages while he 'reads' to himself. He will also know the routines of 'a book at bedtime' and 'We are bored. Let's read a book.'
- By the time your baby is two years old she should be choosing the book she'd like you to read; pointing to the words as you read them in a simple book, and able to dance the hokey-pokey.

CHAPTER 2

TWO TO THREE YEARS

Between the ages of two and three, kids learn:
- what individual words look like
- that words are made up of individual letters
- what letters and syllables look and sound like
- that written words make up different types of books, newspapers, magazines, letters from friends and emails
- how to 'read' a book themselves from left to right by looking at the pictures and remembering the words
- coordination, focusing and language
- how to concentrate on longer stories

Children will still be learning and reinforcing all the things mentioned in the previous chapter — including how to focus and track and what words look like. Don't worry if kids don't *master* all these elements of reading. They probably won't until they are about ten years old.

Don't push kids to learn!

Some kids learn to read at about three years of age; others won't learn until they are eight or nine or even older, and these kids may be just as bright. Introduce these ideas now, but don't worry if they aren't picked up immediately and completely.

Learning shouldn't be restricted to one part of the day or week. If you have words pasted up about the house, books in a pile or on a shelf that kids can reach themselves, a blackboard and chalk or a supply of paper and a tin of pencils for kids to use as they want, then they'll be learning all through the day — and especially when they feel like it.

Let kids choose the books — most of the time

By the time kids are two or three, they have very definite ideas on what they want to read — again and again and again. But they are also hungry to learn about the world. The main problem at this stage isn't that children don't want to learn — it's parental exhaustion!

Let your kids choose the books they want to read, and want you to read to them, from the bookshelf at home and at the library. But add in other books that you like or think will extend their reading and language.

BATTLES AT BEDTIME

If you have more than one child, there may be battles at bedtime about who gets to choose the bedtime book. Put up a schedule for the week: Monday it's Jason's turn, Tuesday it's Emma's turn, and on through the week, with photos of the kids next to their names. Don't forget to give *yourself* a night each week! This teaches kids that (a) parents are people too, and (b) parents love books and have their own favourites to read.

How to read to two- to three-year-olds

Don't push a child to enjoy books that are too complex. You'll soon know if they are bored. If you keep reading a book they don't like, you'll be teaching them that books are hard to understand or boring. But do try to extend the length of the stories you read to them, to help them learn how to concentrate.

Let children read to themselves too. No, they won't be 'reading', but they'll be familiarising themselves with the way the words look as well as checking out the pictures — and learning about which way up to hold a book and page-turning techniques.

Let children 'read' their old favourites in the car (as long as they don't get carsick) or, as with babies, read to them before they go to bed or before they have an afternoon nap or simply during a quiet time. They'll be learning the words as well as having fun.

Cuddle children as you read to them, so that they can see the page and the text easily too. (There are, of course, other reasons for cuddling.)

Sometimes run your finger along the line as you read but not all the time, or it'll be boring for you and may make your child feel that you're not concentrating on them and the story.

Adults are so used to reading that we don't notice all the skills needed. It's not just about knowing what the words say. There's the left-to-right, top-to-bottom layout, not to mention the fact that pages are broken into sentences and paragraphs.

It will be much easier for your children to learn to read if they have understood these factors *long before* they go to school.

Which books to read?

Every day, try to read:

- a familiar, much-loved book

- a new book (one that you've read up to seven times together), and
- one item from a newspaper, magazine, the web or a postcard from a friend.

THE BOOKS THEY LOVE

First of all, read the books they love — even if this means reading *The Cat in the Hat* one thousand, three hundred and ninety-four times. Every time they'll find something new or, just as important, something comforting. Familiar books are also the best way for kids to learn what every word in them looks like. Often that is one of the reasons the child wants the book again — because the book is familiar enough for them to almost read it too.

NEW BOOKS

A 'new' book (this can be from the library) at least once a week teaches kids that the world is full of all sorts of fascinating books, not just *The Cat in the Hat*.

LONGISH COMPLEX STORY BOOKS

These have several lines of text on a page, not just a bright picture and a few words. Read longer books that children will enjoy — this will help them learn to concentrate for longer periods of time. But don't persist if they are bored.

SHORTER BOOKS WITH A FEW WORDS ON EACH PAGE

These shorter books may have an identifying picture, for example, the word *apple* next to a picture of an apple, though they don't have to be alphabet books.

When young children read *Diary of a Wombat*, they pick up the key words in the text even when they are about two or three years old — *slept, ate, morning* — even though some of these might be regarded as complex words.

Most children learn to recognise the words after the fortieth repetition or so. (Yes, OK, reading the same book forty — or one thousand, three hundred and ninety-four — times can be wearing, but whoever said parenthood was easy?)

ARTICLES OR CAPTIONS IN MAGAZINES, NEWSPAPERS OR ON THE WEB

These may interest them, so you can point and say, 'Look, the elephant at the zoo has had a baby.' This teaches kids that reading isn't just about stories, but about real life.

BOOKS ABOUT REAL THINGS

Many people — including many kids — prefer real life to fiction. (I'm married to a man who only reads fiction if it has submarines in it — and they are accurate about the technicalities. But he reads non-fiction widely.) Even by two or three years old, kids may be growing out of the wonder of fictional picture books and want words that explain the world to them. (Others, like me, may love picture books all their lives.)

Good 'real things' books for littlies include:

- kids' books about animals, trucks, dinosaurs, etc.
- recipe books
- popular general magazines, with pictures
- magazines about subjects they like: trucks, motorbikes, food, gardens, sport, houses

(Some two-year-olds are fascinated by bathrooms. The fascination usually doesn't last long, just as the delight in verging on obsession with dinosaurs eventually (mostly) wears off. But while they are in this phase, they'll love a magazine that shows different bathrooms.)

LIFT-THE-FLAP BOOKS
Get children used to participating in reading with lift-the-flap or pull-the-tab books. These also encourage children to really concentrate on the details in books. (Also, they're fun and often beautiful too.)

Reading games for two- to three-year-olds

The key here is 'no pressure', because pressure can cause problems and even slow kids' engagement with reading down. The 'lessons' must be fun. If you're not both enjoying the activity, stop. Some kids want to read when they are around three but others are too busy discovering new things about the world. Other games won't appeal to children until they are three or even six or seven.

Most of the 'games' below are spoken or reading games. Kids of two or three are too young to easily form letters and forcing them to do so may turn them off the idea of writing for a while. The exception here is writing their name — try that with you guiding the pen or pencil, so they have the triumph of putting their name on birthday and other cards.

SOUNDING WORDS

Mum: What's that animal over there, Alex?

Alex: That's a cat.

Mum: (chanting out how the letters sound or singing it to a tune such as 'Twinkle Twinkle Little Star') It's a c-a-t. cc-aa-tt, cat! dd-oo-gg

Alex: Dog!

Mum, clapping: Yay, Alex!

TV WHACKO WORDS

There's no patent on this as I made it up! Feel free to borrow the idea to sell at school fetes.

Make a series of cards with photos of animals, people and other objects cut from magazines. Label each photo clearly — *man, car, bird, cat, dog, house, horse, chair* — vary the words according to whatever the child watches on TV.

The child watches TV with several of the cards in front of her. (Start with one or two cards and add more as reading improves.) If there is a cat on the card (labelled with the word *cat*) she watches for a cat on TV. When she sees a cat she holds up the card and yells, 'Whacko!' and surrenders the card.

The game continues until she is left perhaps with the more difficult cards (e.g., elephant, lion, telephone).

If you don't watch much TV, you can play Window Whacko. Make cards of things the child might see out the window (e.g., grass, sky, car, truck, bus, dog, cat). Don't have cards of exotic things like elephants (unless you *are* likely to see one) otherwise your child will just be disappointed.

MAKE YOUR OWN PICTURE BOOKS

The child tells you the words, you write them down and then he illustrates the pages. Staple the pages together to make a real book. It's easier for a kid to recognise words that they have put into a story.

These homemade books can be alphabet books — A is for *Aidan*, B is for *book* — or storybooks. And then you read the book together.

STOP AND ASK

When you're reading an old favourite, stop at a familiar page and let your child recite the next word or phrase to you. No, she probably won't be reading — just remembering — but it will teach her to look closely at what the words look like and focus on words on the page.

WORD AND LETTER GAMES

Start playing with letters of the alphabet: magnetic letters that can form words on the fridge, letters out of plasticine, big plastic letters or letters cut out of paper or cardboard for children to colour in. Make sure that these are lower-case letters, not capitals. It can be difficult to find lower-case magnetic letters, so you may have to hunt around or make your own.

TEACH CHILDREN THE ALPHABET SONG

The alphabet song is an easy way for children to get to know the alphabet. Once they know the song, make a long chart with all the letters and point to each one as you sing it. After a few weeks let your child point to each letter — and clap loudly when they get one right.

No, learning the alphabet doesn't teach a child to read — although it can be useful for finding things in the library in later life — but it does get them used to which letter is which. Learning the alphabet doesn't even teach children what the letters sound like — C of course sounds like see, not the c in *cat*.

So make it clear to children that letters have sounds as well as names. This is a B and it makes the noise *b* ... *b* ... *b* ... as in *bat* or *big* or *bottom*.

USE WORD CHARTS

Place word charts on doors and in the toilet at child-height. There are excellent alphabet charts available — fruit ones, toy ones, machinery ones. Find or create one that has Australian words like 'biscuit' instead of 'cookie' (an American term). There are also great charts of things like trucks or dinosaurs that aren't linked to the alphabet but just have the word printed next to the item.

Learning whole words

Three-year-old kids may be old enough to learn simple words. This will vary so again — don't push! But they may learn in quite different ways from older kids. Taste and touch may have more impact than what they can see.

EATING YOUR WORDS

The ancient Irish hero Cuchulainn is supposed to have learnt to read using the letters his nurse pressed into his oatcakes before she baked them. Young kids are very interested in what things taste and feel like in their mouths — it's one of their favourite ways of experiencing the world.

You don't have to go as far as the Irish nurse — unless you love baking. But do get kids to 'eat a word' every day, a new word every week. These words can be made from:

- cooked spaghetti with a little sauce;
- scone or biscuit dough (not as good as that means kids eat a biscuit every day)
- apples or other fruit cut into letters and then word shapes
- slices of bread or sandwiches cut into letter shapes.
- Stick to simple words for real things, like *dog*, if you have a dog, or *eat me* — words that have a strong meaning for your child. By the time a kid has eaten a word every day for a week, he'll know that word. After a year, he'll know fifty-two words. After two years, he'll have over a hundred — an excellent basic vocabulary.

Don't expect kids to write or even shape these letters yet. But at the end of the week, let them take the letters and put them in the right order. Don't worry if they can't do it — it doesn't mean they don't know the word, just that they can't put all the bits of it together yet. *Sound out the words as they are eaten, too. C...a...t.*

FEELING WORDS

Young kids learn by touch too. Give children letters to feel. Make them out of fluffy material and paste them onto cardboard. Wrap wool in different colours around cardboard letters or glue fine sandpaper onto them.

Better still, let children help make the letters — and then arrange them alphabetically and into words.

DISPLAY WORDS AROUND THE HOUSE

Write the names of things in your house (e.g., door, bath, bed) on cardboard. This is a great way for kids to learn what many common words look like before they try to read them in a book.

Print big, clear, letters in lower case, not capitals. Stick them appropriately around the house at child-height.

Now and then remove the cards and get your child to return them to the right places. Don't stress about this or make it too challenging and if it's too difficult for your child don't do it. But if she starts getting them right, cheer!

The right time to start doing this is when children enjoy it. If they find it too hard, they aren't ready.

WRITING WORDS

The child tells you the word, you print it and then they colour around it or do an appropriate drawing e.g., cat, house, dinosaur or grandma.

BLACKBOARDS

These are great, as you can use them again and again. If you have two children, or your child often plays with a friend, get a double-sided easel-style one. If you have more than two kids wanting to use the blackboard, paint a length of wall with blackboard paint.

Young kids will mostly want to experiment with shapes and colours by themselves at this age. Let them. They are learning to coordinate their hands and fingers, how to make curved and straight lines. But you can also:

- write their names on the top of the board; and
- write a new simple word at the top of the board every day or every week.

COMPUTERS AND TABLETS

Books aren't just made from paper between covers any more. A book can be read on a computer or other electronic device, and a computer can play much the same role as a book.

Computers are also great for very young kids, because they can write with them without needing to form the letters by hand.

If you don't have a computer, libraries and rural transaction centres will have one that you can use for free or at little cost, although you may have to book time in advance. The local librarian or rural transaction centre manager will help you get started.

Don't be tempted by the costly educational toys that promise to teach your children to read or do arithmetic. Put the money towards a computer instead. Computers do many things; these toys just do one and children soon grow out of them.

COMPUTER GAMES

There are some fantastic educational computer games for very young children that aren't expensive. These games can really help children recognise words, as well as help with focusing, coordination and computer skills — and they are great if, like me, you have a bit of a reading or focusing problem yourself and you don't want to pass this stress on to your children. If you are not sure what some letters should sound like, get the children a computer game.

Reading projects for two- to three-year-olds

MAKE CHRISTMAS AND BIRTHDAY CARDS

Make simple cards from folded cardboard. The child does a drawing on the front and then you write the words for them. This teaches them that they too can produce a piece of written work that someone will treasure and also that spoken words can be written down and recognised by anyone who can read.

WRITE HER NAME

Write the child's name (with one capital letter and the rest lower case) on her artwork, or even on labels, and stick these on her possessions, to teach her that a word can both be spoken and written down.

COLOUR IN LETTERS

Write large 'hollow' letters in short easy words on a blackboard or paper. Get the kids to colour them in.

Games for two- to three-year-olds

Playing games is as important as reading to your children if you want them to find reading easy.

Games aren't just fun; they teach children too. Playing catch teaches children coordination skills and how to take turns. Chasing games teach them how to judge distance, and so on.

Most of the common games when I was a kid were really intense lessons in coordination: bouncing a ball against a wall with one hand and then the other hand, while clapping in between each throw of the ball; playing hopscotch, hopping on one leg and then the other; and skipping. They were all games that taught you how to move in a coordinated way. (Not to mention having fun, cooperating with others and getting some exercise!)

These days so many of the traditional games have been put aside in favour of TV or electronic games. TV is a great babysitter, but it's not a good way to learn. Even educational programs teach kids a few facts or songs or words, not the rich interaction they get from focusing on and imagining in books. Books build brains — TV doesn't.

Try to play at least one game with your child every day. If you can, play one sitting-down game and one active game. (Car journeys are great for sitting-down games.) Encourage children to play games together. You'll have to teach them the rules — these days small families are the norm so there might not be a mob of older children to teach them for you.

GAMES THAT HELP FOCUS AND CONCENTRATION

These are games where children *do* things. Most of these games teach something. (This is not a coincidence — children have most fun when they are learning and being challenged.) Encourage children to play one concentration game and one left–right coordination game every day, with you or with their friends — preferably both!

TREASURE HUNT
Send children to find a brown leaf, then a white stone or a pink shell or flower or a red book, depending on where you are and what they may find. This game encourages visual awareness.

BIG, BIGGER, BIGGEST
Ask children to sort things by size or colour or shape. These can be real things, like blocks or, as they get older, pictures of elephants, cars, buildings and people.

MY GRANDMOTHER'S TRUNK
Each person adds an imaginary item to the trunk and then has to remember all the things that have been

placed in the trunk before their most recent addition. 'I packed my grandmother's trunk and in it I found ... a carrot, an elephant, a chicken sandwich ...'

WHAT'S ON THE TRAY?

An adult (or friend) puts one item on a tray, the child closes his eyes and says what it is. The friend adds another item so there are two, then three, then four and so on — a great way to get children to focus, concentrate, visualise and remember. (Another version is to have half a dozen items on the tray and take one away while the child has her eyes closed. Then she has to guess what's missing.)

SCAVENGER HUNT

Leave a trail of cut-out squares of paper through the house for children to follow, or you could use a trail of arrows stuck to the wall or any other trail (e.g., uncooked pasta or blue wool). Have a prize at the end — a book you will read to them, or a plate of sliced apple.

SING SONGS TOGETHER

Add actions or make up special dances to your favourite songs. This helps kids concentrate, coordinate and remember. And it's fun.

SKIPPING OR HOPSCOTCH
OR FRENCH CRICKET

If you can't remember how to play some of these, find a book on games in the library. These are all excellent left–right coordination games.

Once you put your mind to it, you'll come up with lots of other games that will greatly improve your child's coordination (and possibly greatly help her reading and other learning skills in the process).

COORDINATION GAMES TO PLAY
WHILE YOU WATCH TV

Do your kids *really* want to watch telly?

Parents often assume that their kids want to watch television far more than they really do. When you ask kids, 'Do you always really like watching TV?' most will say, 'A lot of it is boring.'

Kids watch TV because it gives them pleasure without requiring any effort on their parts (just like grown-ups!) and because they don't have anything more interesting to do. Make sure your kids have books to read, paper to draw on, blocks and Lego to build with and lots of other projects. They may choose to do these while they watch telly, or instead of it. But do make sure they have a choice. Otherwise, TV can be a prison, not a gift.

It would be nice if every parent had the time and energy to spend hours each day playing and reading to their kids. In reality, sheer exhaustion means the TV goes on most days.

But television time can also be learning and even reading time.

There are very few shows that need you to concentrate on them all the time. Help kids to play these games *while* they watch TV. And, of course, they can be played with no television, just everyone joining in. All of these games help teach hand–eye coordination. Even better, they teach kids that TV alone can be boring.

BOUNCE THE BALLOON

This is great fun and an excellent way to get children to learn left–right coordination so that they can follow the words easily across the page.

First, blow up a balloon and attach it to a piece of string a metre or so long. Dangle the balloon above the child. If necessary, move the TV so that you can tie the balloon up above them. Kids have to hit the balloon with their right hand, left hand, right foot, left foot, and then twice with their right hand, left hand etc., then three times with each hand and foot and so on.

Balloons are light and *may* be safe to dangle from light fittings (I wouldn't try it). Use your judgement! Curtain rods are safer. You can also tie string between two chairs and dangle the balloon on that, with the child sitting on the ground.

KNUCKLEBONES (OR JACKS)

We used to play this with the knucklebones from a roast leg of lamb but you can now buy plastic ones — or use small plastic blocks. You start with five knuckles (or jacks). You can play many variations of this game but they all involve throwing one (or more) knuckles in the air while picking up or stowing away the remaining knuckles. In one common form of the game you hold a knuckle in your hand and spill the remaining four on the ground. Now, throw a knuckle in the air and before it comes down pick up one of the remaining four knuckles and catch the falling knuckle in your hand. Repeat this throwing and picking up pattern until you have picked up all the knuckles on the ground. Now repeat but pick up two knuckles at a time from the ground. Then three and then all four. Now try it with your left hand. And after that bounce them on the back of each hand, not the palm (much harder). Things can get more and more complex as the game proceeds (eyes shut, clapping between throwing the knuckle up and picking up the ones on the ground, holding the knuckles you have already retrieved between your fingers as you continue to play etc.).

PUNCH AND KICK
The child punches with the right hand, left hand; kicks with the right foot, left foot. this is great for very physically active children.

TAPPING AND STAMPING GAMES
The child taps his head with his right hand, stamps with his right foot, then taps his head with his left hand, stamps with his left foot, taps his nose, chin, neck, shoulders all the way down to his toes, stamping the right or left foot in between each action. See how often your child can do it without making a mistake.

CATCHING A BALL

Teach your child to catch a ball with her right hand, then her left hand, while standing on one leg and then the other. Then play catch with 'silly' things (unbreakable, fairly safe ones such as pillows, cushions, feathers, leaves, T-shirts, rolled-up socks) — great for learning focusing and coordination skills.

BLOCKS, LEGO AND OTHER CONSTRUCTION GAMES

These are good for coordination and fine motor skills.

DANCE

If there is music playing on TV, encourage him to get up and dance!

Work out how your child likes to learn

By two or three years of age, kids are beginning to show the way they prefer to learn about the world. Some kids learn best in a quiet environment. Others like lots of action (kinetic learners), or to discuss things with friends (social learners). When my step-grandson Rory plays on the computer he puts his hands up on either side of his head to block out any distraction. But his sister Emily prefers to do *everything* with as many friends as possible — and if there aren't any other children she arranges her stuffed animals to play the games with her.

Children — and adults — learn in different ways and many may belong to more than one category of learner! There is a lot more in Chapter 8 about this: you can use the descriptions there to help discern what kinds of learning work best for your child. Try to fit the learning games you play into the way she likes to learn — which may not be the way *you* learnt or enjoy learning.

Discovering *how* your child likes to learn now will help you to help them in the years to come.

CHAPTER 3

THREE TO FIVE YEARS

From three years of age children start to learn:
- that words are made up of letters and sounds
- how to recognise simple words
- how simple words can make a sentence on a page
- how to concentrate on even longer stories
- how to form letters of the alphabet
- how to tap out letters on the computer
- how to focus and coordinate
- how to start finding the books they like in libraries, shops etc.

Playing games is still very important (see the coordination and focusing games mentioned earlier).

As children get older, these games will become more sophisticated, but they are still vital. Children need to play a game that involves left–right coordination and a game that needs focus and concentration at least once a day.

A few children will be ready to learn to read now, but other very bright children may not be interested in reading for years. Don't push it! If your kid isn't learning to read, they'll be busy learning other things, even if you're not sure what they are.

How to read to three- to five-year-olds

Let your child hold the book. It's easier to focus on something you hold yourself.

Point to the words as you read them.

As your child gets to know the book — especially if he has asked you to read it four hundred times — ask him to follow the words and your finger with his finger.

When they are confident doing this, ask him to follow the words as you read them without you guiding him.

However ... if your child doesn't like you pointing to the words, or doesn't want to point himself, back off. Otherwise you will be teaching him that books are good for you but not fun.

Spend time discussing the pictures, what people and animals are doing, how they are feeling — *if* your child likes doing this.

Look for the secret ... Lots of superb kids' books have a small secret that kids can discover on the page, like the glorious snail Bruce Whatley put into *Baby Wombat's Week* or the frog in *Emily and the Big Bad Bunyip*. Every kid who finds that snail thinks he is the first person to have ever found it.

Be comfortable. Have a glass of something cool or a mug of something warm within reach, and enjoy yourself. If you're relaxed and happy, you'll be teaching your child that reading is a way to be relaxed and happy. This won't just help make them enthusiastic readers, but it will be a useful strategy for later years when they'll know they can escape stress in a good book.

Reading, not writing

It's much easier for a child to learn to read than it is to learn to write. Writing needs great physical coordination (I still can't write neatly, or even legibly). Reading and writing are two quite separate skills, but we often expect kids to learn them at the same time.

Many children can learn to read a few words or a street sign or a simple book when they are three or four, even though they're not able to write well until much later. But again, let your child tell you when she wants to learn more. If she wants to keep going, let her. If she is bored or, even worse, tearful or stressed because she can't meet your expectations, pull right back.

Children love learning — but only if they are ready to learn and if they enjoy that way of being taught.

Make the whole process as much fun as you can, with appealing coloured or sparkly pens and pencils, whiteboards, blackboards, butcher's paper that you can scrawl all over; you could make letters made out of biscuit dough or cold, cooked spaghetti or 'sandwich words' as mentioned in the last chapter.

How to tell if a child is ready to learn to read

STEP 1. Get hold of a book with simple text, good rhythm and lots of repeated words, like Dr Seuss's *Green Eggs and Ham* or *The Cat in the Hat*, or *Diary of a Wombat* (with Bruce Whatley) or *Dinosaurs Love Cheese* (With Nina Rycroft), or Mem Fox and Judy Horacek's *Where is the Green Sheep?*, or Andy Griffiths and Terry Denton's *The Big Fat Cow that Goes Kapow* or *Brave Dave* or *The Cat on the Mat is Flat* or the wonderful books for early readers by Andrea Faith Potter. These are all very different books, so you can see which one your child wants to use. There are also many, many others to choose from.

STEP 2. Read the book to your child once or twice so that he knows the storyline and can concentrate on other things.

STEP 3. Read the book again, pointing to the words as you go.

STEP 4. Read the book again and again until your child wants another book read or wants to do something else. (Warning: this may take some time.)

STEP 5. Look at your child as you read. Now that she knows the book, is she looking at the pictures or trying to focus on the words? If she's trying to work out a pattern in the words — whacko, it's time to really help her start reading.

How to teach a child to read

See instructions in the next chapter if you think your child is ready: let him proceed at his own pace.

Start at Step 1, and continue for as long as your child is still enjoying himself. If he seems uninterested, the work may be too advanced for him. If he seems bored, the activity may have gone on too long. Children don't like eight-course dinners any more than we do; and their attention span will improve as they get older.

Reading games for three-to five-year-olds

Whether or not your child is ready to learn to read, these games will help them along the path to reading.

SING THE ALPHABET SONG

If you don't know the melody, it should be on at least one of the CDs of kids' songs at your local library. (Plus it's the same tune as 'Twinkle, Twinkle, Little Star', which you might know.) Once kids know the letters of the alphabet, they can play other 'learning word' games.

SING A WORD

Choose an easy but attractive word, like *cat* or *me*. Avoid a lot of the very common words like *the*, *they*, *but*, *very* and *what* because they are too abstract to explain easily to a child. Stick with simple nouns and verbs that are easy to illustrate and use. Now choose a tune, and sing/spell the word to music: 'C ... A ... T ... cat! D ... O ... G ... dog!'

DANCE A WORD

This is the same as above, but add a dance, or clap hands to the rhythm. Many kids learn better if they are moving as they learn, especially when they are young and energetic, and before some of that energy is used playing with lots of other kids at school. Plus, dancing is fun for you and the kids.

THE SIMPLE WORDS WALL

Use a kitchen or family room wall for this, so kids see it often: preferably use the one they face when they are eating. Stick up pictures of simply spelt objects: cat, dog, pig, hat.

Now write their names in lower case (not capital) letters. Now write *the* four times.

Pin the name of the object and *the* under each picture. *The* is there because it is one of the hardest words to work out how to use though it is the most commonly used word. We pronounce it as 'thu' most of the time, not even 'thee'. The sooner kids can recognise *the*, the easier they'll find simple sentences.

Now under *cat* write *sat* and under that *flat, bat, hat* etc. ... all with pictures.

Do the same with the other words. *Dog* gets *log, bog, fog, hog, jog. Pig* gets *big* (several pics of BIG things), *dig. Hat* gets *mat, bat, fat, cat* ... and then you can arrange the words to be as funny as possible. *The hat is a cat*, for example, with a picture of a cat pasted onto someone's head. Yes, this is silly. Kids like silly. If you can think of other simple words with rhymes, use those too.

Every day, run through the words. After a few weeks, ask your child to join in. Don't ask her to read these words until she offers to do so or is saying the right word before you do. Once she begins that, see if she can do it herself. *But don't force the pace.*

RUN AND FIND THE WORDS

Write the names of things you can find in the house: *door, sink, bath, floor, TV, computer*. They don't have to be simple words. N.B. Do not try to Blu-Tack *cat* or *dog* onto a real cat or dog. They may object. But do fix them to a toy dog or cat.

Leave the words there for a few weeks or even months, then point to them, and tell the child what they are.

Now you are ready for the game: you say, 'Dog' and he must run and bring you back the word *dog*.

When he has collected two words, ask him to put them back on the right objects. Don't do more than two at a time or it will be confusing. Start small and start slow.

PICK OUT WORDS ON A KEYBOARD

The child chooses the word, then you hold her hand and pick out that word on the keyboard so she can see it magically appear on the screen. Build up to sentences. If the word is phonically regular (like dog, cat, jump etc.) you can make the sounds of each letter, or groups of letters, as you write them. But remember that many of the most common words (the high-frequency words or sight words) are not phonically regular, so it is not helpful to try to sound them out at this stage. Words like boy, girl, child, mother, father, brother, morning, day, etc., all have to be learnt as whole words.

Again, don't force the pace. If your child just wants to do one word a day, that's fine. Or even play the game once a week. But it does teach her that words are made up of letters, and what they can sound like.

NURSERY RHYMES AND SONGS

Teach children nursery rhymes too, or simple poems, to help them learn how to memorise and concentrate.

MAKE A SENTENCE

Ask kids to say something, for example, 'Our dog is fat.' Write each word on a rectangle of paper and show them how the words go together to make a sentence. Now use the same words to say something else (with another word or two as needed). *My dog is fat* can become *My dog is brown* or *My dog is big*. Then change and add another word, preferably to make something that's fun: *My dog is not pink*, *My dog is not* ... then let the child choose. *My dog is not an elephant*. Keep playing, with variations, until one of you is bored.

RHYMING GAMES

Rhymes are a great way of teaching children patterns in words. Tell them that *cat* rhymes with *mat* and *sat* and your child will work out what *at* sounds and looks like and how the initial letters M and S and C make different sounds.

The more rhyming games you can play with your children the better and you'll probably find that they will start playing them with friends too.

Children catch on to the idea of rhymes very quickly. Children usually pay far more attention to words than adults — after all, a child's main job at this age is learning words!

Say: 'I have a *cat*,

The cat is *fat*.
I have a *dog*,
He's a big fat *hog*.'
... so that your child gets the idea.
Then go on to say:
'Hey, look at *me*,
I've climbed a _ _ _ _ ?'
If they don't say *tree*, suggest *bee*, *sea*, *key*, *me* then *ttttt ... trrrr ...* until they guess the answer.
Other simple lines Include:
'I swam in the *sea*,
And was stung by a b _ _'
Or in the bath you could say:
'Please don't *laugh*,
Jason's having a b _ _ '
As they get more used to this game, just give them the first line:
One, two, three ...
Open the door ...
There is a dog ...
Hi, it's me ...
Don't force these games. If your child isn't ready for them, they'll just look at you blankly or do something else. But if they grin and respond quickly you know you're on the right track.

SAME-LETTER GAMES

The aim of these games is to make children aware of the sounds letters usually make and how they are put together to make words.

For example, help your child find words that start with *b* (not the letter, sound it out): *bee*, *butter*, *bottom*, *banana*. Then find words that begin with *c*: *cat*, *cuddle*, *cry*. And so on.

SIMPLIFIED SOUND I SPY

Play I Spy using initial sounds, not letters. Say, 'I spy with my little eye, something beginning with the sound *d*': dog, dinner, etc. You can play this on and off throughout the day. Concentrate on only one letter every day, so that your child doesn't get too confused. It's also a great game to play when travelling in the car.

Be careful with the sounds you choose. Remember *shop* starts with *sh* not *s*. Keep the sounds as simple as possible. Remember that the English alphabet has twenty-six letters to make forty different sounds so many letters make more than one. And then they are put together two at a time to make *more* single sounds (digraphs — like *ch*, *sh*, *ng*, *th*, ee, ea, ow, etc.).

USING A BLACKBOARD OR WHITEBOARD

Give your child a blackboard (you can buy cheap blackboard paint and create one out of a suitable surface) and chalk or a whiteboard and marker pens and let them play with words. For example, your child draws a picture and you write the words underneath, e.g., *dog*, *house*, *Mum*, *Dad*.

Or you write down a simple word, except for the first letter, and then play I Spy until they guess what the first letter is.

MAKE YOUR FIRST ALPHABET BOOK

There are more complex alphabet books in the next stage and chapter. But this is the simplest: you write a simple word beginning with A, such as apple. Use lower case and choose words where the first letter makes the standard letter sound. *Cheese* or *city* both begin with C but they are not good illustrations of the standard sound that the letter makes: stick with *cat* or *cup*, etc. Colour around the A in red. Now ask your child to draw an apple. Do the same exercise through the alphabet. Choose simple words: bed, cat, dog, egg, fish, go (we go to the supermarket), hop, ink, jam or jump, kangaroo (not simple but fun to draw), lamp, man, nest, orange, pig, quick (someone running), run (the same), sing or sat or swing, TV, umbrella, veranda, window, excellent (with a big X and something your child loves as an illustration), yellow and zoo.

These aren't words to learn or even sounds — see above re letters making many sounds. They are just a way of becoming familiar with each letter.

WRITE A LETTER OR AN EMAIL

Help your child write a letter or an email to a friend or relative. You do the writing, but they tell you what to say. This teaches them how the words they use can go down on paper so that anyone can read them; it will also help them learn to concentrate on a written task.

TALKING BOOKS

Borrow a couple of talking books from your local library when you're going on a long car journey, or to play during a child's rest period when you don't think they are going to sleep but still need some quiet time.

Most talking books don't teach children to follow the words or provide the pleasure of holding a book and reading it, but they do allow children to conjure pictures in their mind about the story and they help teach them to concentrate and listen carefully.

Some talking books, however, come in a set with both a CD and a book, and are told slowly so that children can follow the words.

HOLD LONG CONVERSATIONS

These teach kids about how the world works and encourage concentration too.

DIARIES

Give your child a personal diary. In later years they may want to write their own, but for now you ask them what they do each day, and you write it down for them, adding photos (where possible) and their drawings of what happened.

This gives your child the idea that words can be written down and because they know what the words will be before you write them and they have the photos or drawings to give them context, they'll find it easier to focus on the words and remember what they are.

How to find lots of books without breaking the bank

Books are expensive — especially picture books. Picture books need high-quality, expensive paper to reproduce the colour illustrations and with the best will in the world they really can't be sold cheaply. Often the more beautiful the book, the more expensive it is.

Encourage aunts, uncles, grandparents and other relatives to give your children books instead of toys they already have, or an 'educational' toy that, as has been mentioned, may not educate at all!

But there are ways of getting books cheaply.

- The library. Often. Let your child choose at least half of the books you take out. Don't be afraid to say, 'Mummy/Daddy/Nanna likes this book so we are going to read that too.'
- Hunt for second-hand books at garage sales or thrift shops and if you're lucky you might find a few treasures. And don't be put off if they're tatty: a battered book is usually a loved book.
- Find your nearest second-hand bookshops in the *Yellow Pages* or online. There are fantastic second-hand bookshops — both ones you can go to in person, and others you can browse online — that specialise in 'good' books (and a few bestsellers too) and they often have great children's sections. The books won't be as cheap as those found in a garage

sale, but you may get some treasures and classics that are now out of print but still magic for children.

Avoid movie and TV tie-ins. These books just encourage kids to see the next movie or TV show in the series, not to read another book.

Never throw out a book. Take a box to a second-hand bookshop — you'll get the cash — or better still donate them to the local preschool or primary school — and the books will continue to brighten the minds of even more children. Keep the most cherished ones for the next generation. Anyway, your children would probably howl if you tried to dispose of the books they love. If you give a child a book, it's hers!

When to ask for help
HEARING, VISION OR COORDINATION PROBLEMS

If you think that there may be any problem at all with your child's hearing, vision or coordination, contact your doctor or child health centre straightaway. The sooner any problems are picked up the sooner they can be either corrected or compensated for. For example, if your child doesn't seem able to follow your finger as you skim across the lines when reading, or can't seem to focus on the pictures, then he might well have a problem with his eyesight.

Don't let anyone except a specialist tell you that your child will 'grow out of it'. (Most specialists will also say, 'Here are the things that can help,' even if they have diagnosed that there is no long-term problem.)

Too often parents pick up problems that are dismissed by health professionals who have only spent a short period with a child — not the years that the parents have. If you have any concerns get specialist attention from an optometrist and/or remedial ophthalmologist, an audiologist or remedial audiologist, a speech therapist or an occupational therapist — the latter can really help with children who have problems coordinating or concentrating. The earlier children with problems are helped, the better (see Chapter 8 for further information on seeking professional help).

LOW CONCENTRATION LEVEL

If children can't sit still and listen to *any* story, even their favourite, or they can't concentrate when you give them simple instructions or requests like, 'Would you please get the green mug from the table in the dining room and put it in the kitchen?' then it's worth having them checked, firstly by a GP and then by an occupational therapist. Concentration is something we learn, and some kids need more help to learn it than others.

LATE TALKERS

If your child isn't speaking fluently in sentences by the age of three even when you're at home together without visitors, it's time to consult a speech pathologist. Children who learn to talk late or don't speak clearly are at much higher risk of having learning and reading problems. (But don't expect your children to sound like a university professor — listen to other three-year-olds before you start to worry. And some just like to sit and listen — and may still prefer listening to talking when they are fifty!)

Watch for consistent mistakes in pronunciation, or difficulty making specific sounds or comprehending certain words. If children confuse words, mix up sentences or mix up a story when they are trying to tell it to you, there may be a problem too.

One child I know talked about 'effelents' (elephants) until he was five, but I had no idea until years later that this was an early sign of dyslexia. I still call a suburb of Canberra Wishfick (the rest of the world calls it Fyshwick). Somehow my brain just can't get it straight.

TROUBLE FINDING THE RIGHT WORD

If your child seems to be very advanced and articulate and talks all the time, but has trouble finding particular words or uses long wordy sentences instead of the right words, you should seek help. These children may use the word '*thing*' a lot. They'll know that a word exists for the object they are talking about, but can't remember what it is or how to say it. Again, these children may seem much more advanced than their friends. Ask your family doctor for a referral to a speech and language pathologist.

You don't have to do it all

If, like me, you have reading problems, ask other adults for help reading to your child or, in later years, help with their spelling or other things you find stressful, and get help from computer programs too. But every parent needs help — kids have more energy than we do, to play and learn.

A friend paid a twelve-year-old neighbour to read to her kids for an hour between four and five pm each day. This not only gave her time to get the dinner on, it gave the kids a new person with much more energy to play, talk and read with. It helped 'debounce' them beautifully in time for dinner.

Once nearly all parents had the help of relatives nearby. Now families are scattered. This means that the parents can't get help, *and* it means that people like me long for a bit more baby-cuddling and story-reading than we are able to get from our own families. Ask a neighbour or friend who doesn't have kids over for coffee, then ask if they'd mind reading your child a book while you put the kettle on. If they joyfully grasp both kid and book, you may find you have a potential adopted aunt or uncle.

SKYPE AND PHONE CALLS

My stepdaughter discovered that with a cheap phone plan, she could tell her preschoolers to 'Ring Pa and Jackie' whenever she wanted free time. We had lovely long conversations and she got a break.

Skype is a superb, and cheap, way of being able to see each other while you read a story. If you don't have fast enough upload and download speeds to see each other, even a loved one's voice reading a book is wonderful, especially if you are both holding the same book, even if you are on different sides of the world.

And remember: babysitting doesn't have to be just for when you go out. If you need an afternoon nap or even an evening's work at home, find a babysitter — and give them a stack of books to read to your small ones. (If you can't afford to pay a babysitter, you could ask a nearby friend with kids to look after yours in exchange for you doing the same for him or her another day. Or cook their dinner in exchange.)

CHAPTER 4

HOW TO TEACH BASIC READING

This chapter is just a beginning. It takes years for a baby to learn to speak. It takes years to learn to read fluently. English has lots of weird words and ways to spell and pronounce things.

Once kids have learnt the sounds and words in this chapter, they'll know the basics. As they read books, magazines, text messages, signs, or as they are given other lessons, they will learn more.

You can use this chapter to:

- give kids a head start before they go to school
- help kids who've missed out on learning basic reading catch up to their friends

All the 'learning to read' stages work equally well for young kids or adults.

When to teach a child to read

Your child is ready to read when:

- he tells you what word comes next in a much-loved book
- he picks up a much-loved book to 'read' to himself
- he runs his finger along the text as you read
- he enjoys the 'pre-reading' games in the previous chapters and wants more

Your child needs extra help with reading when:

- she is bored at school
- she is anxious about school and has trouble reading the texts she brings home
- her friends can read better than she can

Kids do learn at different rates, but they choose friends who are pretty much their peers (though sometimes they may not be able to find other kids they have a lot in common with). If your child is falling behind his friends, and school isn't providing him with the help he needs, then it's time for you to help him.

Three steps to reading

STEP 1. The first step is learning what letters and groups of letters sound like. Once a child works out that *c-a-t* is pronounced *cat*, they will find it easy to read the first part of a longer word like *cats* or *catch*, especially if they have learnt what *ch* sounds like. They may even be able to read *mat* and *fat* too.

STEP 2. Putting sounds together to make words.

STEP 3. Learning common words that can't be worked out by sounding them out. Many of these are the most common words, like *the*, *said* and *though*.

HOW LONG DO YOU NEED?

Try to give at least twenty minutes every day. Kids can't absorb much in one go, so don't worry if they begin to fidget after this. But if they are having fun, let them keep going as long as they like.

Do some learning and revising *every* day. That way yesterday's work is not forgotten and kids can reinforce and build on the previous day's skills. *All learning is most effective when it's regular and reliable.*

If you don't have time every day, give them some of the word games in this book to play themselves.

WHEN?

Ten minutes after dinner, but *before* the good-night story. We all remember best if we can sleep on it – that's when memories are cemented into our brains. Or ten minutes before lunch, when kids are debounced after playing outside. Or when you both have time.

How to learn sounds

STEP 1. SPEAK CLEARLY SO THAT THE CHILD CAN HEAR THAT A SIMPLE WORD IS MADE UP OF SOUNDS

Most of us don't speak clearly. It is also hard to hear the sounds in a word if the tv is on, or there are lots of other voices. This seems really simple and basic, but many kids have never heard words said clearly before.

Start with a simple word like *cat*, and get them to say it after you. *c-a-t.* Or look, book. Go on to longer words like *dinosaur. di-no-saur* or apple, banana.

STEP 2. TEACH CHILDREN WHAT THE LETTERS IN THE ALPHABET SOUND LIKE

The easiest way to do this is to make your own 'alphabet book'.

This is best done on a computer, so that the letters will look like the letters they will see on a printed page. If you don't have a computer and printer, go through newspapers and magazines and cut out the letters you need.

The adult writes the letter in both lower case and capitals, then asks the child what words begin with this sound. (Not letter, but sound)

Dad (writing *b* in the book and pronouncing the sound the letter makes — *b* as in *bell*, not the name of the letter): What starts with *b*, Jason?

Jason: B-b-b ... book!

Dad (draws a book): Great! What else starts with *b*?

Jason: Bee!

Dad: Great! (The adult writes the word and the child draws a picture to go with it.)

Some sounds are difficult, like *x* and *y*, so you may need to suggest *excellent* here: 'you are excellent at learning letter sounds!' Or *yummy* with a 'yummy watermelon.'

AN EASY ALPHABET BOOK

This is a list of simple, basic sounds. You don't have to use the words below. Use ones that your child will be familiar with. Ask your child to add others too as they become more confident.

Aa	**Ii**	**Rr**
ant	in	run
Bb	**Jj**	**Ss**
bed	jump	snake
Cc	**Kk**	**Tt**
cat	kid	tree
Dd	**Ll**	**Uu**
dad	lid	up
Ee	**Mm**	**Vv**
egg	me	very (you were
Ff	**Nn**	very good!)
fish	no	**Ww**
Gg	**Oo**	we (we are)
go	on	**Xx**
giggle (tickle	**Pp**	excellent
them for this	pig	**Yy**
one)	**Qq**	yes
Hh	quick	**Zz**
hat		zoo

Learn only one letter a day. The next day go over the letter you learnt the day before, and any other letters you have learnt.

If your child is comfortable with them all, go on to the next letter. It may take a week or longer to learn a letter. Don't hurry! Go at whatever speed your child is comfortable with.

Remember: Praise them! Don't say, 'You should know that by now.'

STEP 3. GO ON TO MORE COMPLICATED SOUNDS

This list teaches kids that letters can make more than one sound. It doesn't have all the sounds we use when we speak, but it has the main ones, as well as the most common words your child will need to know.

Once your child knows these sounds they'll be able to work out words that contain other sounds too.

Learn a new sound each day, as well as revising the sounds you have learnt before.

Mum: What can this sound (points to *a*) do in this word? Ant.

The child then points to the *a* in ant.

Or

Dad: Where can you find this sound (points to the *a*) in this? An apple.

The child points to all the *a* letters.

THE SECOND WORD-BUILDING BOOK

Aa
a ball (a ball and
    an ant)
an apple
are
bath
bag
as (as big as an
    ant)
am

at (we are at
    home)
okay
Bb
big
bag
bath
Cc
cat
child
Dd

dad
duck
do
did
Ee
egg
nest
me
the (the door is
    open)
we (we sit here)

Ff
fat (the cat is fat)
find
fun

Gg
giggle
grin
go
grandpa

Hh
hat
hot
he
his
him

Ii
I (I am me)
is
it
sit
in
if

Jj
jam
jump
jelly

Kk
kid (I am a kid)

Ll
lamb
low
lick

Mm
mmmm (mmmm, I like cheese)
mum
me
my

Nn
no
not (I am not a ninny)

Oo
on (the apple is on the table)
hot
open
over
good
food
gooey (Oh no! Gooey food!)

Pp
pig
pie
put

Qq
queen

Rr
rip
rain

Ss
so
sand
shoe

stink
shall
sing

Tt
table
ten
then
the (ten toys on top of the table)
treasure

Uu
up
yuck
butter

Vv
very

Ww
we
will
was (we saw he was wet)

Yy
you
yes
yap yap yap!
my

Zz
zoo
zip
snooze
buzz

STEP 4. PRACTICE AND PLAY

There are many games you can play to practise finding sounds, or breaking words up into sounds.

How many words can you find that sound like 'cat'?
Cat, bat, fat, hat, mat, pat, sat, that
How many 'b' sounds can you find here? (or 'c' words etc.)
Big bad Bob baked a big bad bun.
Can you find something that begins with 's'?
Sky, sand, sun etc.

You can play this game at any time, even driving in the car or at the supermarket.
Can you see something that begins with 'qu'? queue!
I can see something that begins with b? Big queue!
Can you see a fruit that begins with b? Bananas!
Can you see something that begins with sh? Shelf!

WHAT DOES THIS START WITH?

You can do this either with pictures or with real things. If you have a very active child, play the game when you go for a walk or they are galloping around the yard. It's also a great game to play in the car, as long as you don't have to navigate through traffic or find your way out of a car park.

Dad (points to a dog): 'What sound does that animal start with, Emma?'

Emma: *d*. (This can either be sounded out *d* or, as your child learns their letters, they can say the letter D.)

Once your child has worked out which letter words start with, work on the middle and end sounds.

Dad (pointing to a pool): What's that, Emma?

Emma: A pool.

Dad: What does it begin with?

Emma: P. (This can be either the letter P or the sound *p*, once your child knows what sounds the letters make.)

Dad: Great! And what comes next? What does the middle sound say?

Emma: *oooooo.*

Dad: Great! And what does the end sound say?

Emma: *llllll.*

Dad: Fantastic! Let's write them down. (Dad writes *p-oo-l.*)

STEP 5. PUT THE SOUNDS TOGETHER TO MAKE WORDS

For this activity you need either letters made from plastic, cardboard or biscuit dough (at least two of each letter) or a computer. A computer is better for older children, as it's more 'grown-up' than plastic letters and they don't feel like a baby playing with toys.

Mum: OK, Simon, what letter makes the sound *m*?

Simon: (Picks up the letter or types it. If he selects the wrong one more than twice, go back to the earlier steps and revise.)

> Mum: What letter says *a?*
> Simon: (Chooses the letter or types it.)
> Mum: What letter says *t?*
> Simon: (Chooses the letter.)
> Mum: Now put them all together and you've got ...
> Simon: *m-a-t!* Mat!
> Mum: Wow! Fantastic! Now, what else can you put
> with *at?*
> Simon: *a* ... no, *b! b-at! c! c-at! f! f-at!*

Now choose simple words that you can make using the sounds the child already knows. Make sure the words are ones that sound like their letters. Here are some you can start with.

ant, at, an	nap, nip, no
bat, but	on
cat, can	pat, pet
dog, dad	queen (explain that 'q'
end, egg	needs a friend too, so
fat	it's always 'q and u')
get	rat, run, rip
hat	sun, sat, sip, step
is	tan, tip, top
jam	up
kid (explain that 'c' and	van
'k' are friends and often	wet
sound the same)	(leave x out)
lid	yes, yap
moo, milk, man, mum	zap

STEP 6. PUT 'OTHER BITS' ONTO WORDS

Add 's': cats, dogs, hats, jams, rats, vans.

Ask your child to write a word they already know, then add the 's' and ask what word it is now. By the time you have done this six or ten times they should know it.

STEP 7. LEARN –'ING'

This needs to be learnt as a separate sound. Start with a simple *–ing* word. *Ding! Ping! Ring!* Then add *ing* to other words: *patting, sipping, napping,* explaining that sometimes *ing* needs a friend and you need to double the letter before it.

STEP 8. ADD 'Y'

Learn that you need to double the letter before the 'y'. *Funny, sunny, mummy, daddy.*

STEP 9. PUT LONGER SOUNDS TOGETHER BUT STILL USE SIMPLE WORDS

Even though your child won't know all the sounds, they may still be able to work out the words from the sounds they do know. Try:

alligator	elephant
biggest, battle,	fanning
cannot	grinning
dinosaur	happy

jumping

knit (a good time to explain that sometimes some letters can't be heard)

letter

milky

nonsense

open

queenly

rapid, running, relative

sunny, stitch, satin

tummy, train

this, that, thunder, think, (to teach that 'th' makes its own sound).

tv (to teach that sometimes words don't obey any sensible rule, they just are)

umbrella, under

very

excellent

wombat

zooming

STEP 10. MAKE A MOO BOOK

This is a more complicated sound book and should only be moved onto when your child is comfortable with making simple letter sounds, like *b* and *c*.

It's best to make your own Moo Book, rather than look for a similar book to buy. Most children learn best by doing things, and you'll also be using words that your child knows.

Look for words where two letters together make a different sound from those letters sounded out sequentially. Or where one letter makes a different sound depending on where it comes in a word or the other letters it is near (*y* at the end of a word — *worry*, *family*, etc.; a terminal S that sounds like a Z; the silent-e rule, for words such as *make* or *site*; and r-controlled vowels, in words such as *car*, *girl*, *fork*, etc., for instance.)

These include:

oo as in *moo*	**sh** as in *ship*
ee as in *street*	**kn** as in *knot*
ph as in *phone*	**ng** as in *king*
ou as in *house*	**igh** as in *tight*
th as in *the* or *their*	**ay** as in *play*
ch as in *chop*	**y** as in *family*

Start with words containing 'oo' that make the sound 'oo' as in *moo, boo, goo, loo, roo, woo, shoot, zoo, too,* (explain that this *too* means 'also', and show them *to, too*). Then do some words that sound the same but are spelled differently: *to, do, who*.

Add words that sound the same but have a spelling again: *few, grew, stew, new*.

Now take each of the sounds above and find ones that sound the same and are spelled the same. *ee* in *street* is also in *bee, tree, free,* and many more.

See how many you can both come up with for all the other sounds.

Don't try to do it all

This chapter is the beginning! Your child will need to learn many more sounds. English has all sorts of tricks and traps: how *ck* needs to go together in some words; putting a double letter into *putting* when you add the *ing* and that *ion* is pronounced *shun* as in *attention*! and *ph* can be *f*. And many, many others.

These don't have to be learned all at once. If a child can recognise simple sounds, and knows about 200 common words by sight, they can usually work out other words, especially if they are in a sentence and they can work out what it is in context. It takes a baby years to learn to speak fluently. It takes us years to read fluently too. But the more we do and learn, the easier it gets.

Once a child has the major sounds, and their 200 words, the best way to learn to read is to read.

Read easy books, fun books – your child will slowly learn new words, new sounds, new tricks letters can play, and get quicker and more confident.

Learning the hard words

Many common words are difficult to sound out, like *many*, *hard*, *sound* and *out*. If children learn these common words by sight then it will be easier for them to read sentences. Most of us know about 200–300 of these but difficult words.

COMMON WORDS BOOK
This is like an alphabet book, but instead it uses the words we use in most sentences:

A, an, and	my, mine, yours
the, then, them, than, they	here, there, where
be, by, buy, but	did, do, does
yes, is	put, place
no, not	on, off
never, ever	little, big
can, can't	go, goes, went
will, won't, was	now, then
up, down	mother, father, boy, girl,
said, say	child, children, baby
you, me, us, we	house
him, her, his, hers, theirs	

There are three ways to learn these:

- Write each of these in a sentence on the computer, using simple words the child can work out. i.e. *The cat will go to bed.* Get your child to type out *the* until they fill the page.

- Sing and dance the word. This is fun, especially for active kids. Sing *t-h-e* to a simple tune: *Three Blind Mice* works for this one. Sing *t-h-e*, *the*; *t-h-e*, *the* over and over, dancing or jumping or hopping on one leg or clapping *and* holding up the word printed on a page. If your child doesn't know the names of the letters yet, only the sounds, you can just sing *the* while singing and dancing, but looking at the word the whole time. Or trying to! (This is where the fun part comes into it.)

- Read some funny, simple books together. Because all these words are common words, the child will learn to recognise them as they read the books.

You may need to read the books ten or fifty times before they recognise a word. Luckily there are many kids' books that are great fun to read.

This is where reading a kid's favourite book over and over really helps, because by the time you have read it fifty times they may recognise *the*, *because* and *over*.

Kids also really *work* at working out a word if it is fascinating. Dinosaur, stegosaurus, brontosaurus, crocodile, fairy, doll, bicycle, watermelon: they are all difficult words, but ones that kids want to read.

Learning to recognise words by reading interesting books is the most fun, and most effective, way to learn lots of words.

If you want to teach your child some more difficult but common words, this list will help.

The following list is sorted alphabetically by grade level: k12reader.com/dolch/dolch_alphabetized_by_grade_ with_nouns.pdf

How to teach and read at the same time

Only do this once your child can recognize the sounds that make up words.

Choose a book your child wants to read. Make it a simple, funny book with few words, like *Diary of a Wombat*. Read it to them two or three times, pointing to each word as you read. The next time you read it, point to some easy words and ask them what they are. Next time ask them what some others are. Keep doing this till you think they know most of the words in the book.

Be patient! This may take fifty reads, or more. Finally, read the book together five times. And at last: ask the child to read it themselves, pointing to each word as they read it. If they hesitate, sound the word out for them, or ask them to sound it out. Keep hinting, but let them have the triumph of eventually working out the word.

LEARN WORDS WITH FLASHCARDS

Cut out squares of cardboard. On one side paste a picture and print the word under it. On the other side print the word without the picture.

Start with a set of about six reasonably common but slightly difficult words — the list of high-frequency words will give you plenty to go on with. Don't select long words, just those that you can't sound out easily: *house*, *truck*, *horse*, *cheese*, *honey*. Choose objects that your child really likes — perhaps food, animals or noisy machinery. Don't move on to a new set of words until your child has learnt these.

- If your child is energetic (or even if they're not and need to move more) get them to attach each card text-side up to the matching item in the house or outside.

SENTENCE FLASHCARDS

These are great to help kids learn hard but common words that aren't things they can see or touch.

Write a simple sentence on a flashcard.

Read it out.

Ask the child to draw what is happening on the other side of the card, or to paste on a picture that goes with the words.

When you have at least 20 cards, hold one up and show the picture, then show them the sentence and ask them to read it out.

Useful Flashcard Sentences

(if dinosaurs are not the flavour of the month, use dogs, wombats, horses, fairies, watermelon, or whatever works)

I go through the door with the dinosaur.

I threw a ball at the dinosaur.

There are a few apples left. The dinosaur ate the rest!

The tv is on. The dinosaur is watching tv.

I have enough dinosaurs.

I don't have enough dinosaurs.

I want more dinosaurs.

Help me find my dinosaur.

You are a big dinosaur.

You are a small dinosaur.

They came to play with the dinosaur.

Please can I have a biscuit for the dinosaur?

There is a dinosaur under my bed.

Thank you for the great toy dinosaur.

Can I see the dinosaur again please?

What is wrong with the dinosaur?

What is that? That is an enormous dinosaur!

There are many people here with the dinosaur.

I like dinosaurs.

Do you like dinosaurs?

They like my dinosaur!

Who loves dinosaurs? We do! Do you?

I love dinosaurs.

You like dinosaurs.

Do you like dinosaurs?

The pterodactyl flew here, and there, and everywhere!

Where is the dinosaur?

The dinosaur is under the table.

The dinosaur goes up and down.

HOW TO HELP KIDS WITH FOCUSING PROBLEMS TO 'SEE' A WORD

If your child has problems focusing (test this by asking them to look at a line drawing for ten seconds — if the edges start to blur, then there is a problem) then use a computer to write the word over and over until it fills up half the page, then ask your child to continue writing the word. Then do another page in another font and another in yet another font. Then print out a page of that word and use it as a flashcard.

Don't be in a hurry! If your children only learn one word a week they're doing wonderfully! If you try to push them too quickly they'll either get bored, learn to hate reading, begin to resent you because you keep pushing them, or learn the word of the day by heart (to get you off their case) but not really understand what it looks like.

How to read sentences

The easiest way to go from sounding out a single word to reading sentences is to find a simple book your child wants to read. Read it together, using the steps in this chapter.

You can also write a book together. Kids are rightly proud of their own books, and because they have made it up, they will find it easy to read — even if they use hard to read words like *because*.

Dad: What did we do this morning, Emma?

Emma: We went to the pool.

Dad (writes *We went to the pool.*): What did we do there?

Emma: We had an ice block!

Dad: (writes *We had an ice block.*)

Emma: And I went for a swim.

Dad (writes *Emma went for a swim.*): How's this for a story then? *We went to the pool. We had an ice block. Emma went for a swim.* You read it now.

If your child falters, help them with the first letter of each word.

Emma: *We went to the ...*

Dad: *p ... p ...*

Emma: Pool!

Dad: Yay, Emma!

This also teaches children how to sound out part of the word, so that they can guess what it is by its context.

Once your child is beginning to read more fluently you can try:

Dad (pointing to the letter): OK, Em, what letter does it start with?

Emma: P.

Dad: And what does P say?

Emma: *p.*

Dad: *p ... p ... p ... oo ... oo*

Emma: Pool!

Ways to help a child read a book

Warning: Never read a book or make a child read it just because it will help them learn

to read. We are accidentally teaching kids
that reading is boring, by giving them boring
material to learn to read with.

There are millions of books out there! And at least a thousand that are great to use to teach children to read *and* that will interest your child. When in doubt head to the library and let your child pick out the books they want. Kids may stumble over simple words like *am* and *will* but they'll concentrate as long as it takes to work out *velociraptor* if they are into dinosaurs.

STEP 1. Choose a simple book that you want to read. The library is a great place to find one.

STEP 2. Read the book almost as often as your child would like you to. (No adult can read as often as a child would really like them to.)

STEP 3. Read the book together, pointing at the words.

STEP 4. Read the book together, with the child pointing at the words.

STEP 5. When the child can point to each word as you read it, *and if they know how to sound out words*, stop as you read and ask them what a word is.

Only do this once with every reading, otherwise you'll spoil the story and make it seem like work, not fun.

STEP 6. When your child can confidently read most of the words in the book, ask them to read the book to you. (By now you may have read it 100 times, so it had better be a great book.) Help them sound out any word they don't recognise.

STEP 7. Read another great but simple book ten times at least. Then ask your child if they'd like to read it to themselves. Don't ask them to read it aloud. If they read it to themselves they can skip the words they don't know. Once they have skipped the same word ten times or so they will recognise the word from the context. But *do* be there so they can ask you what a hard word is, like stegosaurus.

READING TO TEDDY OR THE DOG

Teaching something you have just learnt is one of the best ways to cement it in your mind, practise it and understand it more fully. Once a young child has learnt something, ask her if she could teach that skill to the dog or her teddy bear. Older kids — pre-teens or adolescents — can help very young kids master the basics.

How to read bigger books

Kids can read big books as easily as they can read a short book. You just need to tempt them with small bits. Find a book you think they will love. This can be a book you have read to them before. The important bit is that they adore it, or think they will.

Read them the first chapter. This will make them familiar with characters' names and other hard words, like 'volcano'.

Start the second chapter. Stop at a REALLY exciting or funny bit, and say, 'I just have to ...'

Now vanish. Leave the book with them.

If it's a really good book — the sort of book they love — they'll keep reading. Leave for five minutes the first time, then come back and read again. Then stop at yet another tempting spot. Do this until you have both read the book. *But don't ever stop reading to your child* — not until they say, 'It's okay, Mum, Dad, Grandma, Uncle Zachariah, I can read this myself.'

Parents and teachers often stop reading to kids once they learn to read simple books, to encourage them to read more. But they will want more than simple books! If you put them on a diet of only the simple books they can read, they may think that all books are simple, and unsatisfying.

Always have lots of short, easy and funny books around for them to read by themselves. And *always* have a fascinating big book on the go, too, that you are reading to them. Just don't forget to stop at the most exciting bit. Just for five minutes.

Find the magic book

The magic book is the book that lures a child into reading more ... and more ... and more ...

Each kid will have her own 'magic book'. You'll know you've found it when she hugs it close, or doesn't want to stop reading for dinner. For my son it was *Lord of the Rings*. He was far from being a fluent reader, but he *worked* at reading that one. When I was small it was James Michener's *Hawaii*, because my parents didn't want me to read it and it had volcanoes and tsunamis in it. (They were right. I had volcano and tsunami nightmares for years — do not give your kids this book.)

Some kids love funny books. Others — serious kids who'll turn into serious adults — find these frivolous or plain silly.

Some kids love sad and even tragic books — the pages of their perfect books have wrinkles from copious tears that are shed each time they read and reread their favourite books, whether they are *Black Beauty* or *The Diary of Anne Frank*.

Others love books about animals or cars, or rockets and space travel. Others love books about children living lives a bit like their own; others love books about children leading lives nothing like their own!

Some adore books set in the past or another culture, or in the future and on another planet.

There are children who love myths and legends from many countries. And others who want to read only about things and situations that are 'real'.

When in doubt, take them to the library and let them graze. If it's boring, stop reading. Books are not like broccoli. They may be good for you, but you don't need to eat every bit on your plate.

If a book is boring, encourage kids to put it down *and get another one*. And another and another, all kinds of books, till they meet the right one, and fall in love.

CHAPTER 5

HELPING WITH READING

Learning to read takes time, but it should be fun, too. Here's how to help.

The four Rs: Regular, Revise, Relax and Reward

REGULAR: A LITTLE EVERY DAY

When kids are learning to read it is easy for them to forget what they have learnt if it isn't reinforced the next day. Go for 'little and often'.

REVISE

Go back over at least some of yesterday's work before you move on to anything new.

RELAX

Tempt but don't force. If your child doesn't want to read then you have the wrong book ... or the wrong time (i.e., when they really need some time out for themselves or a game with a friend).

Kids can get to a stage where they can read to themselves, which is faster and more fun than reading aloud. Just be there if they need to ask.

REWARD: THE WORK IS ITS OWN REWARD

Don't promise bicycles or an extra hour of TV in exchange for success. Give sincere and heartfelt praise, not rewards, except for the rewards that come as a direct result of reading: books, and more books, visits to the library, subscriptions to their favourite magazines. Let them browse in the newsagent — with supervision — to find one they like.

A step-by-step guide

STEP 1.

Read the first paragraph or even the first page to the child, so they get the feel of the story and know difficult words like 'volcano' and characters' names. Names are often a real sticking point, even when children are becoming quite competent readers, so 'introducing' the characters is a good strategy (not everyone has a phonically regular name like Ben or Kate or Jim these days!) for any beginning reader. Then:

STEP 2.

Ask the child to read a sentence. If this works, ask the child to keep on reading. If they need to be prompted more than once or twice in a paragraph, keep reading alternate sentences, so the story progresses fast enough to be fun and comprehensible.

STEP 3.

Help, don't tell. If your child doesn't know a word:

- encourage them to sound it out using their knowledge of letter sounds
- if they can't sound it out, begin to sound it out for them. Stop after the first sound, and see if they can go on from there. Then add another sound ... and another ...

If you have to make every sound for them, still wait for them to put all the sounds together. Try not to jump in — beginning readers are sometimes able to put all the information together to make the correct word if they are given sufficient time to do it in.

STEP 4.

Encourage. Every time they work out a hard word, congratulate them. Make a list of praise phrases, and use them often. But be sincere, be honest and be reasonable. Don't say, 'You are the brightest kid in the class' unless you have verified evidence that it's so. The exception to this is any over-the-top phrase: 'You're the most brilliant reader in the entire universe' is OK, as is 'You read faster than a velociraptor can run.' Many children love high fives or some applause and, if they are your own children, a hug or a kiss. Just let them know how delighted you are with both their efforts and their progress (these may not be the same!).

You can't read if you don't have a book

Many kids with reading problems in schools have no access to books at home. Kids need to go home with a book. And, yes, in some homes, books will disappear or be damaged. Better a damaged book than a more damaged kid.

Even better is if they see reading behaviour modelled at home — when the only person in the household who is expected to read is the beginning reader it feels very foreign and odd to them. If every member of the household is seen to read, sometimes for information and sometimes for pleasure, it becomes a normal activity that all people do. Whether it's noticing Dad reading the manual for the vacuum cleaner or looking up a fishing report or reading poetry or Mum looking up a word or catching up on news or with her nose in a novel and older siblings engrossed in the latest sci-fi or horse book — all these serve as subtle (or not so subtle) clues that this reading caper is enjoyable, valuable and (almost) universal.

Entrancing 'learn to read' books for all ages

Learning to read will be boring if kids are given boring things to read — and too often they are. Reading material needs to be so fascinating that your child will focus utterly on working out what comes next.

Each kid needs books they are fascinated by. I've tried to do this with several of my series for young people, but there are many, many other superb books.

Many authors — and I'm one — have deliberately written books to entrance beginning readers. But often the 'magic book' — see page 88 — will be a difficult one, not an easy one. And it's not always easy to know at first what kind of books a child will like.

So you need to ASK. Kids may be too embarrassed to say, 'I'm bored with this book.' They may even think that books are always boring. Ask, 'Is this book fun?' and if they say 'No' or are too polite to say no but mumble, 'I guess ...' or something else a bit evasive and less than wholehearted take it as a no and offer others. Remember most children very quickly learn that you would like them to like books and read — and they don't want to be rude or hurt your feelings. So, even if it was your absolute favourite top-shelf book when you were young, do not be offended or put out if they have other ideas about what they want to spend time and energy on.

LEARN-TO-READ BOOKS FOR LITTLIES

Anything by Dr Seuss

Anything by A.A. Milne

Andrea Faith Potter's 'ten-word books': to read these first five books, you only have to be able to read ten words. shop.andreafaithpotter.com

The Cat on the Mat is Flat by Andy Griffiths and Terry Denton

Where is the Green Sheep? by Mem Fox and Judy Horacek

The Terrible Suitcase by Emma Allen and Freya Blackwood

I'm a Dirty Dinosaur by Janeen Brian and Anne James

Splat the Cat by Rob Scotton

Feathers for Phoebe by Rod Clement

Rudie Nudie by Emma Quay

Goodnight, Mice! by Frances Watts and Judy Watson

The Fearsome, Frightening, Ferocious Box by Frances
    Watson and David Legge
I Got this Hat by Jol and Kate Temple, and Jon Foye
There's a Hippopotamus on Our Roof Eating Cake by
    Hazel Edwards
The Little House by Virginia Lee Burton
Caps for Sale by Esphyr Slobodkina
The Story about Ping by Marjorie Flack
The Very Hungry Caterpillar by Eric Carle
Where the Wild Things Are by Maurice Sendak
Goodnight, Moon by Margaret Wise Brown
Meg and Mog books by Helen Nicoll and illustrated by
    Jan Pienkowski
The Journey Home by Alison Lester
Yellow is my Favourite Colour by Judy Horacek
Are You My Mother? and *Go Dog Go!* by P.D. Eastman
Dinosaurs Love Cheese by Jackie French and Nina
    Rycroft
Good Dog Hank by Jackie French and Nina Rycroft
The Hairy-Nosed Wombats Find a New Home by
    Jackie French and Sue deGenarro
Pete the Sheep (age three and upwards) by Jackie
    French and Bruce Whatley
Looking for Crabs by Bruce Whatley

PICTURE BOOKS FOR FIVE- TO EIGHT-YEAR-OLDS
The Pros and Cons of Being a Frog, Sue deGenarro

Too many Elephants in this House by Ursula Dubosarsky and Andrew Joyner
Cloudy with a Chance of Meatballs by Judi Barrett
Diary of a Wombat by Jackie French and Bruce Whatley
Wombat Goes to School by Jackie French and Bruce Whatley
Pete the Sheep by Jackie French and Bruce Whatley
Josephine Wants to Dance by Jackie French and Bruce Whatley
The Mog books by Judith Kerr
Anything illustrated by Julie Vivas

BOOKS FOR FIVE TO TEN-YEAR-OLDS

The *Selby* and *Emily Eyefinger* series by Duncan Ball
The *Tashi* series by Anna and Barbara Fienberg
The *Tree House* series by Andy Griffiths and Terry Denton
Charlotte's Web by E.B. White
Charlie and the Chocolate Factory by Roald Dahl
Pippi Longstocking by Astrid Lindgren
Finn Family Moomintroll series by Tove Jansson
The Secret Histories (Barney Bean and Elsie books) by Jackie French
The Phaery Named Phredde series by Jackie French
The Wacky Family series Jackie French and Stephen Michael King
The Bugalugs Bum Thief by Tim Winton

NON-FICTION

The Dorling Kindersley DK series on everything from trucks, cars and motorbikes to cookbooks, horse books, dinosaurs etc.

The *Women's Weekly* Cooking Guides (complete with many glossy pictures)

Also think dinosaurs; anything slinky slimy or scaly; dogs; and fairies. Any good guides to frogs, snakes, volcanoes, etc., even if they are aimed at adults, usually have large pics and little text.

Non-fiction can be particularly great for kids with low self-esteem: they get to tell everyone else about the universe.

CARTOONS AND GRAPHIC NOVELS

These usually have minimal text but lots of illustrations to show what's happening. They appeal to everyone from five-year-olds to adults.

Footrot Flats, Murray Ball

Asterix the Gaul series by René Goscinny and Albert Uderzo

The Tintin series by Hergé

TEENAGERS

Tomorrow When the War Began series by John Marsden

Eric by Shaun Tan

Rules of Summer by Shaun Tan (warning: nightmare
     potential)
In fact anything by Shaun Tan (including *The Arrival*,
     which has no text at all)
Jandamarra by Mark Greenwood and Terry Denton
Harry Potter series by J.K. Rowling
The Narnia series by C.S. Lewis
The Hobbit and *The Lord of the Rings* by
     J.R.R. Tolkien
His Dark Materials series by Philip Pullman
The Sally Lockhart series by Philip Pullman
Anything by Robyn Klein
Anything by Sonya Hartnett
The Matilda series by Jackie French for girls; *Oracle*,
     Hitler's Daughter or *Pennies for Hitler* for boys.
     But I've had letters from kids who have suddenly
     discovered they loved reading when they've
     accidentally come across a broad range of my
     books, sometimes more difficult ones like *Refuge*.

AND FOR HORSE-MAD KIDS
The Silver Brumby series by Elyne Mitchell
The My Friend Flicka trilogy by Mary O'Hara
Anything by Marguerite Henry but particularly *Misty
     of Chincoteague*
The Penny Pollard series by Robin Klein

CHAPTER 6

HANDWRITING AND SPELLING

Helping with handwriting

Learning to write is one of the hardest tasks we will ever do. You not only have to know what letter to write, you have to concentrate to make it the right shape, in the right spot on a page. It's much easier for kids to learn to write on a computer, where they just have to press on the right key to make a letter appear, instead of shaping it for themselves on a page.

A twelve-year-old girl I met last year couldn't even write a sentence — she thought. But when I told the group of kids she was in to 'just write and keep on writing and no one needs to read it' (a great way to get kids creating fluently) she scribbled page after page with all the rest. At the end of the workshop she came up shyly and asked me to look at her work. It was superb — a fascinating story. I was reading the second page before I realised that she had begun each line randomly at either the left or the right of the page.

I'm dyslexic. I read in chunks, not from left to right. Her way of writing made no difference to my ability to read her text. But it did to her — and nearly everyone else who read it.

'I don't know where to start on the page,' she said.

I told her that computers do that for you. You type and the computer program places the words along the line and then when it reaches the end of that line it begins at the right place on the next line. She looked both incredulous and overjoyed. 'Really?'

The principal asked her, 'Would you like to try writing on the computer in my office?'

The girl nodded. Two hours later she was still typing — and still crying with joy. If only she had been taught to write on a computer she wouldn't have missed seven years of literacy. (The next step was to teach her touch typing.)

HOW TO BEGIN

- Make sure your child has a pencil that fits his hand comfortably. A very thick one may be hard to hold, and a thin one too difficult to coordinate.

- Show him how to hold a pencil.
- Give him lined paper to begin with, but also use a ruler to mark out diagonal lines very faintly to help him get the right slope to the letters.
- If your child presses too hard, and many in their anxiety do, buy some carbon paper at the newsagent. Put it under his work to show him that you don't need to press so hard to make a mark.
- Tell your child to *pull* not *push* the pencil across the page. Write a few words and you'll see what I mean. Left-handed children may find it hard to pull unless they twist their hand around. Give them pencils that flow easily across the page to make writing easier — make sure the pencil they are using is an HB or softer. All pencils are graded — H stands for Hard and B for Blackness so to make a good mark without needing to use undue pressure the pencil needs to be either HB, B or 2B or even softer. In fact do this for right-handed children too!

SHAPING THE LETTERS

- Write words as neatly as you can or, even better, print them out at a suitable (large) size in neutral font from the computer.
- Put tracing paper over that page and ask your child to trace the words.

- When they have traced the words a few times, ask them to write the words themselves.

It's more important for a child to learn to read and write (or type) early than it is for them to develop copperplate writing.

How to help with spelling

This is a confession. I can't spell. My solution to this is to use the spellcheck tool in my word-processing program; and I have a friend who corrects my work for me and turns a mess into a manuscript.

Trouble with spelling — real trouble, not just 'I can't be bothered I want to watch TV' trouble — may be a symptom of other problems.

Is your child having trouble hearing the sounds in each word?

Is she having problems focusing on the words? Or breaking the words up into parts? Or putting the parts back together? Or ... Well, I could write another book on this subject alone.

If possible, seek expert advice from a special-education teacher to work out which part of the spelling process is the problem.

Don't try to teach them too many spelling rules at once! Let your child practise examples of one rule for a few minutes every couple of days for two weeks before going on to another rule. A little spelling practice every day or every second day works best rather than a great whack at weekends, as your child gets bored or frustrated because she can't concentrate that long.

Always revise a few words before you add new ones and try to make the activity sessions interesting: combine a few methods each time and always include one fun session, e.g., spelling with water pistols, singing a new word, playing Word Snap, using a computer or sprinkling hundreds and thousands into word shapes.

BREAK WORDS INTO CHUNKS

Ask children to say words clearly, emphasising all the sounds. Make sure that they can pronounce each word correctly and pronounce every syllable in the word, e.g., *beau-ti-ful*, *ex-cel-lent*.

Then ask them to use coloured pencils to find little words in big words. Finding the 'on' in 'conceive' and circling it in red can help children break the word down into more manageable bits.

> Make letters out of cardboard (or biscuit dough or cut-up rockmelon)
> Ask children to add endings (suffixes) to words: *make, makes, making.* Or they could add beginnings (prefixes): *remake.* (You'll find common prefixes and suffixes in any good dictionary.)

- Sing the spellings of difficult words to silly tunes, over and over until children learn them like a song.
- Write difficult words six times with a water pistol on six different surfaces — the garage wall, the front path, the patio floor, the bath, the shower curtain, the front steps, etc. No, not on their little brother. Unless he agrees to let you use his back. The sillier the place the word is written, the more likely it is that your child will never forget how it is spelt.
- Give kids lists of words that have the same combinations of letters and sounds, so they learn that these all follow the same rule: *train, pain, brain, main, again; tree, keen, bee, fee, green.*

USE WORD ASSOCIATIONS

If kids find a particular word hard, show them how to find a clever way to remember it.

- **pigeon**: Help! There's a pig being chased by a *pigeon*.
- **write**: Write a 'w' when you write.
- **kick**: Make the 'k' into a picture of a child kicking.

When all else fails, tap dance or stomp out the spelling twelve times. Music uses a different part of the brain from speech. Often if you sing and dance it, you'll get it.

I can spell 'encyclopedia' (the American way!) because I sang it once a week with the Mickey Mouse Club on TV for a year. I can spell 'receive' because Grandma danced me around the room as we sang it. Once again, if you learn one word a week, that makes fifty-two words in a year, and a whole vocabulary in five years.

SOME USEFUL SPELLING RULES

1. I before E except after C. Provide examples: *receive*, *ceiling*, as opposed to *believe*, *fierce*, *friend*, etc. But also explain that the way we talk and spell changes all the time with new words and new rules and it isn't always sensible, so there are lots of words where E comes before I nowhere near a C like *their*, *either*, *foreign*, *feisty*, *leisure*, *height*, *seize* and so on, and there are some after C exceptions like *science*, *sufficient*, *ancient*, *efficient*, etc.

2. The fairy E (often called the silent E). When there's an E at the end of a word, it makes the vowel in the word say its own name, so *rat* becomes *rate* because the fairy E makes the A say its own name. And *cut* becomes *cute*, *hat* becomes *hate*, *kit* becomes *kite*, *not* becomes *note* (the vowels are A, E, I, O and U).

3. When two vowels go walking, the first one does the talking. So in *dream* you say the letter name E, in *road* you say the letter name O.

4. Drop the E if you add an —ing, so *hope* becomes *hoping*.

5. A little vowel means that you need two of the next letter to build up a word. So skip becomes skipping because the little I makes P get a friend.

AND USE THE SPELLCHECK ...

The spellcheck is the world's greatest spelling teacher.

After half a century of being unable to spell, I finally began to learn how ... by using my spellcheck. It hasn't been fast — and I still can't tell if a word is spelt correctly, or not at a casual glance — but I have at least discovered that I never spelt 'Australia' the right way, or 'also' or 'veranda', and did finally work out what I was doing wrong.

Using a spellcheck not only corrects your work: it teaches you, as you have to choose from several words that look much the same (or at least they do to someone for whom spelling is a challenge!). My spellcheck is even — slowly — teaching me to focus on the individual letter components of my words.

Give me another fifty years and I may not even need a spellcheck ...

CHAPTER 7

HOMEWORK, ESSAYS AND STORIES

How to write an essay (a beginner's guide)

Most people know how to write an essay: they just don't have the confidence to do it. When you tell your friend what you did last weekend, you are creating an essay. You begin at the most relevant spot and give a brief overview of what happened — 'So did I tell you about how we made meringues even though Mum said we weren't allowed to?' You work through the detail and build up to a conclusion '... but we got it all cleared up and we had like forty meringues and she didn't see a thing.'

Last year I met a 'slow learners' group of teenagers who were convinced that they couldn't write an essay about *Romeo and Juliet*. (They're the ones whose teachers had moaned in the staffroom about how 'hopeless they all were, the lot them' and 'I don't know why we turn up, some days'. And, as an aside, I don't know why they turned up either.

These kids all had excellent insights into the play — they'd hated it ('all those words') until they'd seen the movie. Then they had realised that it didn't read well, but was absolutely magic when performed. They could analyse each scene ...

I scribbled down what they said, word for word, and showed it to them: instant essay, and one that should get a high mark.

They were astounded. Why had no one ever told them how easy it was? Possibly because those someones were too busy moaning in the staffroom that they didn't know why they bothered to turn up.

If you — or your child — can explain something to another person, then you can write it down, exactly the same way. Then go through it, divide it into paragraphs ... and there you are — one essay.

Most essay problems come from trying too hard, and from thinking that what you've noticed about the subject isn't smart or academic or original enough to impress a marker. It's easy enough, once you have confidence in your observations, to put them in the order a teacher wants to see. Tell the whole story in a few sentences; go to town on detail in the middle; then tell the story again to finish it off. As the song says, just stick to 'Doin' What Comes Naturally' and you'll be fine.

If ...

And this is a big if.

If you know what you want to say — and know your subject — it will be easy to write.

If you don't know what you want to say, and are trying to work it out as you go or are covering up the fact you don't have much to say — you'll end up with a mess.

So:

STEP 1. Work out what you want to say.

STEP 2. Scribble down a few points, and I do mean 'scribble'.

STEP 3. Work out a brief summary of what you want to say.

STEP 4. Pretend you are telling it to your best friend. Write it down, just as you'd say it.

STEP 5. Divide into paragraphs and whoosh it round a bit — and make sure the first paragraph gives a good idea what the rest will say and that there's nothing new in the last paragraph.

STEP 6. The last paragraph should sum up what you've written, or what you've learnt from it, or be the end of the 'story'.

If the ideas are good, the essay will be good. If you don't have any inspiring ideas, keep thinking till you do.

How to write stories

I met Gavin at a high school. I'd been asked to give a workshop for the keenest creative writing students and Gavin, who was definitely not in the top set, asked the librarian if he could come too. She asked me if I minded having one more student join the group and I said, 'Whacko, the more the better.'

Gavin didn't participate in the workshop but he didn't look bored either. He frowned now and then as if he were working things out, and then nodded with enormous concentration. He stayed behind when the others left and asked if I'd mind having a look at his story. I said I would, expecting a few pages to peruse. He fished out a great wad of paper from his sports bag.

I blinked.

'It's only eighty-six thousand words so far,' he said. 'I think I'm about a third of the way through. I wrote another story last holidays that was one hundred and twenty thousand words, but this one is better.'

I began reading. On the first page there was one decapitation and a space carrier with all its passengers blown up. No more murders until page three.

'I didn't want to show it to any of the teachers,' he said. 'They'd think I was weird. I want to write books like Stephen King when I leave school.'

It was brilliant writing — clear, direct, well-paced. OK, it was full of blood and sex, but there was nothing so kinky, nothing so dark that I was afraid he was writing to work out some horror at home.

This child just liked a good, bloodthirsty thriller — a taste shared by a large part of the male (and a smaller but still significant proportion of the female) population — and could write one of his own well enough to be a multimillionaire when I'm eighty and counting my cents to see if I can buy an extra scone.

His story wasn't at a professional standard yet — you don't get that sort of polish at fourteen — but at the rate he was writing, and really working at his writing, I expect to see his work on the airport bookshop shelves within a few years.

I tried to persuade him to show his teachers; he refused. I had a chat to his teachers and told them what he'd written and why he hadn't shown it to them. One said automatically, 'Well, he was probably right. I don't see why boys want to write that stuff.' But by the end of lunch the rest of us had convinced her otherwise.

Why expect children to write 'nice' stories when they don't want to read 'nice' books or watch 'nice' movies, and their taste is so widely shared?

I hope that the teachers encouraged him to show them his work. I think they must have. He hasn't emailed me his new book so I suppose he has another audience and helpers now. But I do sometimes wonder how many other kids are bored and under-performing because they are expected to be something they are not.

What kids get from writing stories

Fun. Writing stories is like riding a bicycle — hard work at first, but once you are used to it and good at it, it's delightful!

Word skills. They discover how to use words they've heard and put words together in good and evocative combinations.

How to think clearly and consecutively and put thoughts in the best order for people to understand them. Even if your child stops writing fiction at twelve, he'll have learnt skills that will help him write anything from a work email to a report to an instruction manual to a critical essay.

Empathy. Every time you create a character and think about their motivation, you are learning to understand how others feel.

Compassion. Once you feel as others feel, you may even be more inclined to 'do unto others as you would have them do unto you'.

Focus and concentration. You need to hold a world in your head and juggle bits of it.

Creativity. Jogging creates leg muscles. The more you jog, the better your muscles. The more you create, the better your creativity becomes. Kids who learn to create stories probably won't write them when they are adults. But they will be better able to create a visionary business plan, a new theory of sub-atomic particles, a new app, or a cost-effective method to capture and use CO_2 from the atmosphere.

Fun.

Fun.

Creating a story step by step

STEP 1. THE THINKING

Thinking is the most important part of writing a story. A badly written story with fascinating ideas will be fun to read. But even the best writing in the world can't make boring ideas into a good book.

The first idea for a story that kids come up with is usually based on a book they've read (or listened to) or movie that they've seen — pretty much a cliché. But the more they *think* about their story the more original their idea becomes. And the better it gets, the easier and faster it is to write.

When kids are first learning to write stories it often helps to do so in a group — the whole class works on it together the first time, then maybe a group of friends continue to thrash it all out.

Ask kids the answers to these questions. (They don't need to write them down. Once they know the answers the story builds up in their minds.)

- Where is the most fascinating spot in the universe to put a story? The place you'd LOVE to be now? A beach? A volcano?
- Is it nearby? Is it another country? Is it another planet?
- What does it look like? Sound like? Smell like?
- Think of three absolutely fascinating things to put in your story.
- Who are the main characters? Think of their names.
- Are they male or female? What species — humans, animals, aliens, mermaids, vampires, zombies?

- How old are they? Babies, kids, teenagers, twenties, thirties, or extremely elderly?
- What do they look like?
- What do they spend most of their time doing?
- And — most importantly — what do they want more than anything else in the world? Will they have it by the end of the story?
- *How does this story end?*
- And ... what else needs to go in this book to get to the end?

N.B. Kids don't have to stick to the outline they create when they first think of the story. It's not a recipe. It's just a way to get them thinking by responding to a series of questions. The more they think the better and easier it's going to be to actually write it. *Of course* the story will change as they write it, or get other good ideas. Here's an example of thinking out a story.

Phase A. Where would the best story you have ever read be set? I'd set mine in a world with intelligent wombats who served scones and jam and cream down wombat holes. But you might prefer a story set on a spaceship, or a zombie world where everyone lives in giant zombie chickens. The wombat holes are as big as a town hall; the soil is bright purple, pink or green, and all the furniture is made of baked mud. Purple soil smells of chocolate. Pink soil smells like watermelon. And green soil smells like dog doo.

Phase B. Who are the main characters? I'd have the world's most handsome wombat, Fuzztop. And a vampire chicken called Gloria. Who would your main characters be?

Phase C. Three things you really love and want to see in a book: macadamia ice cream, lots of cold watermelon and zombie spaghetti, a terrifying treasure hidden deep under the earth, a battle between the furry forces of good (the wombats) and the Slime Worms of the Dreadful Depths Below.

Phase D. How the story ends: Gloria learns how to vampirise a carrot. Fuzztop invents The Way of the Carrot — a new form of martial arts using vegetables. The Slime Worms turn out to be allergic to carrots, which is good as The Way of the Carrot may be delicious but it's not much good for smiting non-allergic Slime Worms. The world is saved, apart from the carrots, as now Gloria is eating them too. And the treasure turns out to be … So try it for yourself. Where is the story set? Who are the main characters? Three things you'd love to see in a book (or more —

a good book needs a hundred great ideas, not just three). How does the story end?

STEP 2. WRITE THE MOST EXCITING OR INTERESTING BIT
But, and here's the catch, don't stop writing till you've finished it. Doesn't matter if it's messy or not as good as it could be. Just write! (This is to astonish reluctant writers ... they will be stunned and delighted at how much they have written, and how good it is if they've had fun thinking up a great story first.)

STEP 3. WRITE THE ENDING
Don't worry about spelling or punctuation.

STEP 4. NOW WRITE SOME MORE BITS

STEP 5. PUT THE BITS TOGETHER
Add any other bits that are needed ... rewrite boring bits ...

(But be aware that Step 5 may not happen for years. Most of the stories kids come up with are for long novels or a TV series — not a short story, but they only have time to write a short story. Pushing them to 'finish' the book will only make them hurry the story along. It teaches them bad writing. Best to make sure they finish writing the ending and leave the 'complete' stories till they are older and have a spare year or two.)

P.S. Few adult writers can write a good short story. It's harder — not easier — to stun the reader with a few words instead of lots. The short story is the hardest thing you can get kids to write. A fragment of a long story is infinitely easier.

How to make your stories better

(Taken from my *How the Aliens from Alpha Centauri Invaded My Maths Class and Turned Me Into a Writer ... and How You Can Be One Too*, Harper Collins, July 1998)

HOW TO AVOID MOTH-EATEN IDEAS

Have you ever had a second-hand jumper? OK — second-hand clothes are always just a little bit faded — and the more they're used the more faded they become.

Second-hand ideas are like that as well. If you base a story on something you've seen on TV or a book you've read, it'll always be just a bit faded too — no matter how bright and exciting the original was. It's the same with second-hand images — if someone says to you 'it was as hot as hell yesterday' you don't cringe away in terror. Except you should — after all, it's a *horrifying* image if you really think about it — heat like the fires of hell, so great your flesh is melting off your bones ... but the point is you *don't* think about it because you've heard it so many times before.

The first person who heard that expression probably *was* shocked ... but now it's not just second-hand, it's millionth-hand — and it's faded. Very faded. It just doesn't mean much any more.

So what can you say instead? OK — what do *you* know that's hot? Chips sizzling in the frying pan, bitumen that oozes through your toes, the car roof so sun-baked you can fry an egg on it? (Do *not* try this at home — I know a kid who did and the stain's still there five years later.)

And if you want an original character — one that hasn't mooched out of a book or movie ... well, that's why you need to learn to make compost.

But that's another story.

HOW I MAKE MY STORIES FAT

If an alien from Alpha Centauri were travelling over the earth right now and looked through my window at me at the computer, then looked through your window at you — what would they say is the main difference between me and you?

OK, I'm an adult and you're a kid — but maybe aliens think that young humans are really caterpillars and we don't get two legs till we're older.

The alien might notice that I have brown hair and green eyes (I don't know what colour your eyes and hair are), or that I'm dressed differently (I bet you're not wearing a skirt with flour smudges, a T-shirt with blackberry stains down the front and bare feet) or that I've got a scar on my left hand where a wombat bit me. I'm not sure how observant aliens are.

But there's one thing the alien would notice straightaway ...

I'm fatter than you are — and my stories are much, much fatter than your stories.

If you want to write good stories you need to make them fat. Skinny stories are no use at all. *Everyone* writes skinny stories when they start writing — you get an idea between your teeth and run with it as fast as you can till the end because you want to finish as fast as you can — because it's exciting, because it's interesting or just because the sooner you get the blasted thing written you can go and do something else.

So you're writing skinny stories.

A skinny story is like saying: ... *and then the dragon ate the knight and all that was left was his armour and his bones.*

That's a really skinny story — and it's boring because it's skinny.

Instead of saying ... *and then the dragon ate the knight and all that was left was his armour and his bones* you need to tell the reader ...

What did it feel like inside the knight's armour?

What could he see?

What did the dragon's breath smell like?

What did it feel like in those last few seconds as the dragon's teeth penetrated through the steel?

What did the bones smell like three weeks later?

What did the dragon feel like when her stomach was full of knight? (Maybe he hadn't washed for six months and she got indigestion.)

When you write a story you have to put *everything* into it. You know what that world is like in your mind — but the reader only knows what you've put on the page.

So make your stories fatter.

Once you've made them fat you have to make them skinny again. This is one of the secrets of really good writing.

When you make a story skinny you go through and cross out *everything* that's boring — because if it bores you, it'll bore everyone else. You have to cross out any words that don't say much. (Most verys and lovelys and awfuls don't mean much ... it's better to put down exactly what you mean. Instead of — *It was a lovely day* say *the day was bright as chilled butter.* Instead of saying *I felt awful*, say *My cheeks were so red I thought I'd frizzle up and disappear ... but I didn't, more's the pity.*

Go through your story and look at *every* word — and see if you can use a better one. (Not too complicated, though, because if people have to stop when they're reading and say to themselves 'Ah, that's an interesting word — I wonder what it means' the spell's broken. Use simple words if you can.)

When you make your story skinny you have to go through and pull out every word you can get rid of — most *ands* and *thens* and *wases.*

And by now you're probably yawning and thinking, I don't care what she says, it sounds like a lot of work.

Well, it isn't. This is the way to write your stories fast — much faster than if you didn't make them fat then make them skinny.

As I said before, most of the time you think you're writing a story you're just sitting there thinking, What am I going to say, what am I going to say? No, that won't work. *Help*! I can't think what to say ...

When you know that eventually you're going to go over your work and cross out everything that doesn't work you can just start writing — and keep writing even if it's rubbish. It doesn't matter because you can cross it out later. So you write fast, and faster, and faster, and faster ...

Once you learn to make your fat stories skinny — really chop out bits and add bits and rewrite bits — you'll find you just start writing and keep going till you can't hold the pen any more.

BOOKS THAT GALLOP: SLOWING YOUR STORIES DOWN

When most people get an idea for a story they start writing and gallop away with it, trying to finish it as soon as possible.

Well, of course. It's exciting — so you want to get to the end. Or the teacher's waiting for it so you have to finish it.

But hurrying a story makes it a bad story.

Consider this bit of writing for example: ... *and then we raced up the castle stairs and grabbed the treasure from the dragon and escaped out the secret tunnel.*

That's a boring bit of writing — because it's too fast. There isn't any time to build up suspense.

And then we crawled closer, closer, closer to the dragon.
The dragon twitched its nose.
We froze.

'Do you think ...?' whispered Michael.
His voice broke off as the dragon opened one
round and golden eye.

It's boring when a bus goes slowly, but when a story goes slowly it's more exciting, because you have more time to wonder what's going to happen next.

Slowing stories down also gives you time to get to know the characters in the story. Who cares what happened to the kids in the first bit of writing? I'm not going to start snivelling if the dragon crunches up their bones. They're strangers. But if I've lived through the story with them for ten or twelve pages — or even two pages — then I'll be turning the last page in a hurry to make sure they're safe.

Long stories are usually more effective than short stories. (Not always. But it's very difficult to write a *very* short story that still has the power to move or excite readers, or be remembered by them years later.)

Always make your stories as long as you can. Most of the time you won't be able to make them very long — you won't have time. But if you can write a little bit of a long book instead of trying to cram all the ideas in your head into a few pages it will be a better story — because that way you won't get into the habit of writing books that gallop.

AN EXERCISE

Tell your best friend the most exciting thing that has ever happened to you.

But don't just say, 'The most exciting thing that ever happened to me was when I fell off the roller coaster at Wonderland.'

That's a skinny story.

Make it fat. Take *ten minutes* to tell how you fell from the roller coaster at Wonderland (or were almost eaten by a shark or run over by a semi-trailer ...)

What were you doing on the roller coaster? Why were you there? Who were you with? What did it feel like? Look like? Smell like? How come you fell? What did it feel like flying through the sky? What could you see, hear, smell? What was everyone else doing? What did it feel like when you landed?

Now you've got a fat story. And a heck of a good yarn you can tell over and over again ...

Some issues people have with writing

WHAT MAKES A GREAT BOOK?

It's not only the way it's written — though that is important. *It's the ideas.* A great book needs a great story. You don't need a good idea for a story. You need a hundred and twenty *great* ideas. And you have them. Anyone who doesn't have fascinating ideas is a slug pretending to be human. You just need to dig them out. See the steps earlier in the chapter to help with the digging.

I CAN'T FINISH MY STORIES!

If you are under twenty, don't worry. You probably don't have time or brain space due to school; and also your writing ideas will be changing and developing very quickly. It's probably best to write lots of bits of stories, rather than work on one long one, so you can play with ideas and ways of using words. If you hurry a book or story to finish it you'll be teaching yourself very bad writing habits that will be difficult to break. (One of the most common faults beginning writers make is to hurry their stories, and do too much in them too fast.)

But if you just come to a stop in a story, you haven't really thought about it enough, so go for a walk, or listen to music for an hour with three apples or a very large hunk of watermelon and just *think* about it. You may know that you need to change your story — or do a heck of a lot more work to it — and you can't bring yourself to do it.

Accept that the better the book, the more sheer hard work it will involve. Take a deep breath and do what the book needs. You may be scared it won't be as good as it should be. Well, it probably won't be. Doesn't matter. Just write it — then you can rewrite and rewrite and rewrite. It is much easier to work with something already down on paper than something in your head. So get writing — but be prepared to trash it when it doesn't work.

I CAN'T GET ANY IDEAS!

There is no such thing as inspiration! Just years of *thinking* and looking and listening and analysing — then suddenly it all comes together and you know what your story is going to be about. And then you *really* start thinking. Yes, there is a point when a story idea comes together — but if you haven't done lots of thinking about all sorts of things first, it won't happen.

Ideas don't just drift out of the sky. I wish they did. They have to be worked for. So ... what are you really interested in? (If you say, 'Nothing' then there is no way you are going to be a writer.)

Think about the last two weeks — what did you feel excited about? And, yes, this can be as simple as playing with your dog — write a doggy book — or gossiping with friends. Write about what you care about. Think about the most vivid scene you can create in your mind. Your own home? An alien planet? A tropical island? That is where you set your book. See the extract on page 119 from *How the Aliens ...* for more on outlining a story.

MY IDEAS ARE LIKE THE LAST MOVIE I WATCHED OR BOOK I READ!

See above. Stories need thinking about. You can't spin a story out of nothing, no matter how brilliant you are with words. If your ideas are always second-hand ones, stop being lazy and *work* at your writing.

P.S. I'm an amateur violin player. I love playing, but not enough to practise. Amateur writers write because it's fun, but they don't love it enough to work and sweat at it. I'm not saying you have to be a professional writer — you will get enormous pleasure being an amateur writer, and give pleasure to others too, not to mention finding/developing useful skills. But if you want to be a good writer, you need to put a heck of a lot of work into it — at least as much as if you wanted to become a doctor or teacher. Talent is not enough!

I DON'T KNOW WHERE TO START!

Write the ending first. I'm serious. It's easy to write the beginning of a story — then stop, as you run out of ideas, but if you write the ending first you have to *think* about the story. What is it about? Who is it about? What do they want more than anything else? Will they find it? Where will this story end up? You may not stick to the ending. But it *will* make you think before you write.

P.S. It's much easier to write a good beginning when you've already written some of the book. The beginning is the bit that will haul the reader in — so it must be vivid. But just because it will be read first doesn't mean that it has to be written first.

MY TEACHER HATES MY STORIES!

No one has ever written a story that all the world loves. And, also, teachers sometimes think kids shouldn't write books with sex, swords or any of the other things you'll see in most movies or read in just about every popular fiction book. But don't worry about it too much. You'll have another teacher next year; and even though it doesn't seem like it, school days do pass. And then you'll be able to write what you want … and find you have to please a hundred thousand people and not just your teacher!

HOW CAN I WRITE THE BEST STORY?

Think about your story before you write it, no matter how good your writing is.

And don't over write. It took me years to realise that being good with words can actually be a handicap if you want to be a good writer! I'm very good with words. I can make words stand on their heads and wiggle their toes. But beautiful writing doesn't make a good story. *Ideas* make a good story — and if the story itself isn't good, no amount of good writing will make it interesting. Sometimes too people who are good with words over write — they use more words than they need to tell the story. *Use as few words as you can, even if every one of them is beautiful.* Words can really get in the way of the story. (On the other hand someone who is brilliant with words can weave a story out of almost nothing ... but that's *almost* nothing: the story must be there, and the words will just be doing a perfect job of telling it.)

P.S. If the reader ever stops to think, Hey, wow, isn't that expression wonderful? you have failed as a writer. A writer's job is to get the reader so involved in the world they are creating that they are aware of nothing else — even the words used to create the story. Stunning writing should only be obvious when the reader has already read the story at least three times and can now concentrate on how the book was made.

How to get kids to love writing stories

The best way to show kids how much fun it is to create a story is to do it as a group, together, making the story as outrageous and funny as you can (see above). Teachers and parents often accidentally convince kids that their stories must be meaningful or beautiful. Beautiful meaningful stories are good things to have. But most people like to read — and write — fun ones.

Kids need to be given the freedom to write the kind of stories they like to read. But just like someone who loves a hunk of watermelon may like a gourmet meal too, kids who start writing 'silly' stories may find they grow to love writing the deep and meaningfuls, too. And a book can be deep, meaningful and also fun.

A list of Don'ts

DON'T CENSOR

If you find yourself saying 'I don't think that is a nice thing to write about. Why not ...?' stop at once. Instead accept their idea, but subtly, carefully, encourage them to focus on their other ideas so the one you are uncomfortable with slips away. But do think about why you don't like the idea before you do this. Sometimes we have a double standard and expect books and stories written by kids to be 'nicer' than the things we let them watch on TV.

DON'T USE STORIES AS A SPELLING TEST

If someone stopped me every time I made a spelling mistake I'd never have finished writing a page. (But you can sneakily make a note of what they can't spell to work on later. Just don't tell them where you found the words.)

DON'T MAKE KIDS FINISH THE STORIES
THEY ARE WRITING FOR FUN

You will just make them hurry the story along. If they want to write professionally, they will discover very quickly that a story must be finished. Till then, let them experiment. Kids' writing styles evolve so fast that making them keep writing one story may prevent them from leaping to the next level of creativity with a new idea.

DON'T SET A WORD LENGTH

Most ideas for stories are for novels or movie scripts. They need at least seventy thousand words, not five hundred. Again, a target such as this encourages kids to hurry their story along. And once again, they are accidentally being taught a lousy writing style. One day, when they have time, they may finish a book — if they want to. If they wanted to be a builder you wouldn't expect them to build a whole house at their age — just experiment with building other things. So don't expect them to write a whole book either.

ASK THEM TO WRITE THE FINAL SCENE OF THEIR STORY

This makes kids *think* about their story: you can't write the final bit without working out where it begins, who the characters are and much else. And the final scene of a book often makes an excellent short story.

A SHORT STORY IS ONE OF THE MOST DIFFICULT GENRES TO WRITE WELL

And we expect kids to do it! Instead, ask for a beginning scene, a final scene, and a 'vignette': a dramatic or moving scene somewhere else in their story. That's it. Finish.

LET THEM RANGE!
Let your children write about what *they* want to write about — this is fun, not a way to turn them into a junior Shakespeare. And if they *do* turn into a junior Shakespeare they are best left to experiment and find their own voice.

DON'T WORRY IF IT'S A LOUSY STORY!
Of course it will be lousy — they are just beginners! But also the more ambitious a young writer is, the more experiments they'll try. Kids who write 'nice' stories — a bit like their latest favourite book and with butterflies in the margin — are possibly just trying to please their loving parents, not writing from the heart. Give them the freedom to make a mess of it!

DON'T REWRITE
This is often done by teachers or parents to make the story better. Sometimes it makes the story worse, adding 'overwriting' and distorting what was a clear simple story. But mostly, when a kid, or an adult, writes a story it is *theirs*. You can suggest how *they* can change it. But remember it is their property, not yours. And yes, you can probably make it better. But

that won't teach them how to write a better story. It will just dampen their confidence; it will make them feel that there is a right and wrong way to write a story (There isn't. Every great writer breaks 'rules' of writing.) It will teach them that writing is work, not fun. Actually writing *is* work. But in the words of Terry Pratchett, it is also the most fun you can have by yourself.

PROVIDE PAPER OR A WORD PROCESSOR
Sounds obvious, but how many houses have writing materials on hand? And when a kid wants to write they want to do it *now*! Leave piles of scrap paper where they can be found easily and used whenever the child wants to.

PRAISE THEM!
No, they are not Margaret Atwood or Tim Winton — yet. There will nevertheless be something there that you can pinpoint as commendable. So praise that and them and their hard work. Make the praise really concrete and particular — not a general, 'That's great!' Find some element or passage in the writing that you can single out and comment on so that they know you have really bothered to read and notice what they've written. Too often children are fobbed off with platitudes and broad statements when what

they really want is to know that they are worthy of your undivided attention and focus.

IF THEY ARE REALLY INTO WRITING, BORROW BOOKS ON WRITING STORIES FROM THE LIBRARY

See *How the Aliens from Alpha Centauri Invaded My Maths Class and Turned Me into a Writer and How You Can Be One Too*, a book written to encourage kids to write. But reassure them that every writer has his or her own ways of making up a story. I outline my stories and think about them for ages before I start the actual process of writing, that is, putting words on paper (or, rather, on screen!). But other authors find that boring — they'd rather just write and not know what happens next until they have written it! In other words, give kids help and support — but leave them free to do it their own way too — or to find out which way works for them.

GIVE KIDS A GREAT RANGE OF BOOKS TO READ AND SAMPLE

This will help them to absorb the techniques other writers have used to say the things they want to express.

DON'T TRY TO GET THE WORK PUBLISHED

Kids can write brilliant stuff — but it's usually only ninety-eight per cent brilliant. And that uncertain, amateurish two per cent will almost certainly make publishers reject the book and disappoint your child.

A kid who wants to be a doctor doesn't expect to start practising at fourteen — and it's a really bad idea to let him think he might be a professional writer at fourteen too. (The mother of Nobel Prize winner Patrick White paid for his early poems to be published, and in later years Patrick White did his best to get hold of every copy still extant so that he could destroy them. The stuff you write at fourteen, even if you are brilliant, may be extremely embarrassing ten or twenty years on.)

On the other hand, a kid's story can be a great gift for aunts, uncles and doting grandparents — and a great memory to hand on to their own kids in twenty years or so too. There are computer programs that will let you produce a reasonably professional-looking book. Or ask for the advice of one of the companies that specialise in self-published books. Contact the Writers' Centre in your nearest capital city for a list.

On no account pay for your child's book to be self-published then pretend that a publishing house has published it and that they are a 'real writer'. Of course they *are* a real writer — but a novice, unpublished one. Paying for your child's book to be published then calling a media conference about your genius offspring is a good way to destroy her confidence, because as the years go by — and you can no longer buy them a brilliant HSC result, university experience or career — they are going to feel that their life is heading downwards, not up into the heights of genius you said they had.

Ask yourself why you want him to be published. Because it makes you feel great you have a brilliant child? Be patient. A brilliant child will grow into a brilliant adult — if he is not pushed so hard and high he comes crashing down. But if the book is printed for the family he will see how it's treasured not just because it's great, but because he is himself loved. Which is worth a million small grabs in the local paper about a ten-year-old 'published author'.

Helping with homework

Don't nag kids to do their homework — *help*! But not by doing it: by making it easier for them to do it. (See 'Signs you are helicoptering' on page 219). If your child has a problem, and asks for help, then help her solve that problem. But don't do the work for her: show her how to do it herself so she learns how to cope with pressure and deadlines. She'll need those skills in the years to come.

- Make homework time good, not bad: give them a quiet place to do it, with good lighting and no interruptions. Schoolwork is *difficult* and kids need the same good working conditions as an adult might expect.

- Don't use bribes — let them enjoy work and achievement for their own sake. Don't say, 'If you get eighty per cent this year I'll give you a bicycle.' But do use unexpected rewards — 'Hey, you did so fantastically I want to give you this!'
- Often though simply celebrating an achievement is better than a gift — a celebratory dinner, with the table set formally and their choice of tucker and toasts, 'To Egbert!'
- Celebrate small successes — don't make your child feel they have to achieve some far-off goal to be congratulated. A week of really working at their homework, a teacher thanking her for a useful contribution in class, an improvement in *anything* — all are worth cheering!
- Having a child really working at something is more of an achievement than high marks — doing our best is rare for most of us!
- Be wary of hollow, empty praise. Make praise specific not general. Instead of saying, 'You're just a fantastic all-round kid,' focus in on a specific achievement. 'I really like the way you have coloured in that heading' or 'That story you wrote about the visit to Grandma's is so good that I feel we should

send her a copy — but I really want to keep the original!'

Kids have very sensitive radars when it comes to anything remotely insincere and if they think you are trying to manipulate them with bland, one-size-fits-all praise it will undermine their confidence even more.

Don't overpraise either. Even if you are pretty sure your kid is a genius, don't tell her. If she doesn't turn out to be a genius, she'll just feel she's failed. And if she *is* a genius she won't believe you; she'll wait till her efforts are recognised by the outside world.

- Don't *you* stress over homework! I used to find this impossible, especially with spelling and maths. They were both such tortures for me that I am sure I passed on my stress to my son — my body language was shrieking: Oh help, we are in for a nightmare here …

  I finally discovered that I needed help, i.e., someone else to help my son with his maths. Don't get stressed if you don't know the answer! Ask. Ring a friend — yours or theirs. Ring a relative. As a last resort, see if you can hire a tutor on retainer, to pay them every time your child needs to call them and say, 'How do you …?'

- Do other learning things together, so they learn that learning is good for its own sake not because it's a part of school or because you'll be punished if you don't do it.

It can be really good for them to see you cope with the inevitable frustrations that come with learning any new skill. So do something challenging together — build a balsa-wood model plane or glider, set up a tropical fish tank, make a pair of overalls — it doesn't matter what the project is, rather that you do it together and that it is a challenge for both of you.

This allows them to see that you keep on learning all your life and that even difficult or new activities bring enormous pleasure once you have invested some time and energy into mastering the basic skills.

If you have a problem with frustration and anger management yourself, do something about it now. Don't model fury as a response to meeting an obstacle to your child — adult tantrum throwers are even less attractive than child tantrum throwers.

Make Christmas cards together or build your own radio kits or make a bookcase or find out how to keep bees (assuming that neither of you is allergic to bee stings) or how to keep chooks or grow avocados or whatever other fruit your child loves. Life is about learning, or relearning is about life, whichever way you put it, and school is only a small part of that.

CHAPTER 8

READING PROBLEMS AND TEACHING PROBLEMS: AND HOW TO HELP

Many kids diagnosed with reading problems learn in different ways from most other kids: they may need to move as they learn (kinetic learners), talk about what they have learnt (social learners) and the other ways discussed below.

These kids don't have a learning problem. They have a teaching problem. They need teaching methods that fit the way they learn.

Other kids may have problems at home or with bullying, or health problems ranging from a toothache to sleep apnoea which means they don't get enough sleep. These kids need extra help at school till the problem is sorted, but don't necessarily need different approaches to learning or teaching.

Other kids *do* have learning problems: ear, eye, coordination or other problems that mean they can't follow lessons as easily as other kids. This doesn't mean they are dumb, or even slow learners — these kids are as intelligent as their classmates, generally, and many have above-average or even very high intelligence.

But it does mean they too need to be taught in different ways from most other kids.

KIDS MAY BE DOING OK AT SCHOOL AND STILL
HAVE A LEARNING PROBLEM.

A very bright dyslexic kid may manage to pass each course, but he'll still be frustrated and bored. Some of the most disruptive kids are the bright ones who have a learning problem, either one like dyslexia or one caused by a home problem. Often if you can get a kid fascinated in his schoolwork and proud that he is doing well, the disruptive behaviour will vanish. (But not always.)

How to tell if kids have learning problems

- They can't read as well as their friends or other children in their class, even though they seem as bright as the others.

- They aren't doing as well as their best friend. Kids tend to choose friends who are pretty close to them in ability. If your child is markedly behind where her best friend is in literacy and general schoolwork it can be an indicator that all is not well on the learning front.

- They're frustrated by not being able to learn fast enough. It's normal for every child at some stage to yell, 'No! No! I'll never learn my five-times table! My life is ruined!' But if this happens often there's either a learning problem or they're being pressured too hard to succeed.

- They don't read as well as you think they should, even though they are keeping up with the rest of the class. Be careful with this one. It's normal to feel that your child is a genius, but you don't always need to worry that he's an under-achieving genius if he doesn't get outstanding results. (Hey, he just might be normal!)

- They reverse letters, especially bs and ds, even long after their initial introductory efforts. Ask a child to write the word *bed* or copy it from your writing to see if they can manage b and d yet. (A good way to teach which way b and d point is to show children that the word bed makes a bed-shaped word. You can even write a lovely big version of bed with a small person lying on the bed to help your child remember which way around these letters sit.) Kids may also write their words inside out or back to front.

- They skip words or lines when they read or write, or find it difficult to find the beginning of the next line as they read down a page.
- Their spelling is inconsistent, even though they can read and write fluently.
- If when they stare at a word or a simple drawing the outline becomes fuzzy after ten seconds or less there is probably another problem.

The first great dyslexia myth

All too many people — including a surprising number of teachers — think that if a kid *doesn't* reverse her bs and ds she is not dyslexic.

This is rubbish.

If you come across people who think that, gently try to correct them. If it's your child's teacher, and he or she isn't prepared to learn more about learning problems, move your child to another class, or another school, and write a calm but firm letter to the principal and school board, asking that teachers be given extra support to learn more about reading difficulties. Perhaps one kid in eleven has a reading problem — and that means one teacher can convince a lot of kids they are stupid.

The second great dyslexia myth

'Dyslexia' has become a grab word for a wide range of problems. Too often some twit studies a group of people with reading problems and makes generalisations about dyslexics. Be wary of any study that groups all people with reading problems under the one label. Not all students with reading problems have dyslexia. Not all dyslexics have reading problems. I can't follow a map, but I am an extraordinarily fast reader. Nor is there any one definition of dyslexia: it can cover everything from problems visualising words and letters to tracking or remembering them, and hundreds of other permutations.

Dyslexia is a convenience word. It means you are better at speaking words than reading words. That's it. Researchers are still arguing about whether dyslexics have verbal, visual or coordination problems. I suspect that the answer is that dyslexics can have any of those problems, or maybe other ones, or just see the world differently so what may be a 'problem' at school can be an advantage in other ways.

Other dyslexia myths debunked

- Dyslexics don't all have visual problems and many won't be helped by coloured glasses and visual aids.
- Dyslexics don't all have problems hearing and understanding words. Many are unusually gifted in this area.

- Dyslexics don't all have below-average intelligence. The only way a researcher may believe this is true is if they only study dyslexic kids who are failing at school. Dyslexics are often — but not always — above average in intelligence, and sometimes brilliant.

Kids who learn differently

These are the kids with a *teaching* problem: they need to be taught in another way to learn most efficiently.

No two humans process information in exactly the same way. And we don't learn to read in the same way either.

My husband, Bryan, loves diagrams. I get lost in car parks. I zap out half a dozen books a year. He takes three days to write a birthday card (or gets me to dictate the words). Bryan can understand a wiring or software diagram in the blink of an eye.

Bryan is a visual learner. I am a verbal learner. When we watch a movie together Bryan is always saying, 'Hey, did you see that?' and I say, 'No.' But he can never understand how I can follow the movie and write a letter at the same time. If I dash out to the kitchen to put the kettle on, as long as I can hear what's going on, I'm fine.

In school Bryan learnt what was written on the board; he probably missed half of what the teacher said, but if it was written up on the board he was fine. I mostly daydreamed out the window, but as long as the teacher kept on talking, I still followed what was going on.

Humans learn in various ways:

- Visual learners
- Verbal learners
- Physical or kinetic learners
- From our sense of touch and smell (tactile or olfactory)
- From interactions with other people (social)
- And probably many other ways as well!

Most of us process information using a combination of these various ways; others are very strongly slanted towards one means of information processing over all the others.

Most kids do best with a range of learning techniques in the classroom: some talking, some writing on the blackboard, some group projects, some physical projects. It makes school more interesting if it's varied. Other kids only learn well in *one* way, not *many*.

If your child fits strongly into one of the following categories, they may need extra help learning in the way that fits them best.

Visual learners

A visual learner needs to *see* things, not hear things. They need things written down. Phonics are harder for visual learners to grasp.

These children are often very bright indeed. That can be a problem, because their intelligence masks the *real* problem and that problem can mask their intelligence, so they get frustrated.

Visual learners often don't do well in the early years of school, when they are struggling to learn the basics, but they often speed ahead in high school once they've grasped what they need to get going.

HOW TO TELL IF CHILDREN ARE VISUAL LEARNERS

- They love computers, diagrams, machines, and how things work. They often love computers, graphics, TV, doodles and music.
- They are far more sensitive to noise, distractions, light, colour and the sheer intensity of sensual experience than other children.
- They are often extremely good at problem solving.
- They are very creative and excellent at analysis.
- They don't 'hear' when you ask them to do something. Many kids are good at 'not hearing' when you tell them to tidy their room, but visual kids especially need to learn to concentrate on what they hear/is being said.

- They are easily distracted and like quiet to focus on their computer (or whatever is absorbing them at the time).
- They are much brighter than their schoolwork results suggest. (Although this can be the case for children with other problems too.)
- They have very vivid imaginations.
- They often have vivid and disturbing dreams.
- They are often very distracted by things happening out the window or at the back of the class.
- They can have more difficulty with times-tables and spelling than written work, although if those tables and spelling lists are made visually interesting with graphics and colour this can help.
- They can be very disorganised in some things, and organise themselves superbly in other things, i.e., they know exactly what drawings they have done, or what computer games they have, but forget they have swimming on Thursdays.
- Often they forget their homework or what they are supposed to be doing in class; they wander off task.
- Sometimes when you talk to these kids it's almost as though it's another language — they pick up bits of it but not enough to make sense.

WHAT TO DO

- Ask the teacher to use a lapel microphone while your child uses headphones streaming the teacher's voice and cancelling out classroom noise, so they are not distracted by what's happening around them.
- Concentrate on the sight method where they learn to recognise whole words, as well as phonics. Yes, they'll still need some phonics, but using flashcards and reading books over and over with the child looking over your shoulder until they recognise the words and the way they fall into patterns will probably teach them more.
- Use a computer as much as possible to teach your child the steps of how to read in Chapter 4, so that they can *see* all the steps written down.
- Let them do as much homework as possible on the computer too.

Verbal, auditory or sound learners

These are kids who learn best from things they hear, not things they see. In extreme cases these children — and adults — can't retain the image of what a word looks like in their mind for long enough to learn it. (But this is very rare.)

Verbal learners though shouldn't be confused with fast processors (see page 154). Fast processors have problems with many visual things, but are very good indeed at others. I can't read a street map properly, but can absorb a contour map at a glance, seeing the map as the landscape it represents. I find it hard to read a single word, but easy to scan a page in a couple of seconds.

HOW TO TELL IF A CHILD IS A VERBAL LEARNER

- Ask the child to look at a word, a single letter or a simple black-and-white sketch. If it blurs within ten seconds, they have a problem focusing and will have learnt to gather information about the world mostly from what they hear, not from what they see. (I can only look at a word for a fraction of a second before it blurs.)
- They hate diagrams and find it difficult to focus on written words.
- They don't like computer games, jigsaws, Meccano or anything you have to look at to solve.
- They misread assessment questions or homework instructions.
- They'll talk a lot, or love listening to others.
- They love analysing people and their motives.
- When young, they do far better at oral work than written work.

WHAT TO DO

- Some kids may be natural verbal learners. Others may have a physical problem. Work out *why* they are having problems focusing on things. It may just be something they are born with, but it may also be a symptom of an eye problem (or another illness). Have your child examined by your family doctor and ask whether they think the problem needs to be investigated further. If necessary, ask for a referral to an ophthalmologist who specialises in focusing problems. They may also need exercises to help them coordinate, focus and track across the page.

- Give the child a laptop computer. Touch typing is essential, so they don't have to look at what they write. Kids as young as three or four can learn to touch type. Once they are familiar with written letters and words, it is far easier for them to learn to read.

- Help children learn to focus on words so that they start to know what they look like. Have them trace over the words with a finger or a pencil or copy text from a page onto a word processor while they say the word at the same time. They only need do this a few times until they know what the words look like.

- If you suspect your child may have a visual problem when they are under five, give them cut-out fuzzy letters to feel, food shaped as letters and words to eat, so they learn in other ways.

- Kids with severe visual problems — and this includes visual processing as well as loss of sight — can learn to read Braille. For some kids, learning Braille can help them learn to read using their sight once they are confident Braille readers.

The hints below for fast processors will also work.

Fast processors

This is the form of dyslexia I have and it seems to be one of the most common forms of learning difficulty. We need to do things *fast* or not at all.

Fast processors have to process information quickly or they don't process it at all.

Some children with this problem can learn to read before they go to school by the word recognition method, but many others don't.

These children tend to be much brighter than average. For this reason they may also be disruptive in class as they're bored. Their confidence is easily destroyed too. These children *know* that they are brighter than their friends, yet they can't manage even the simplest schoolwork their friends fly through.

Many famous dyslexics fall into this group. Some have never learnt to read, but have achieved much despite it.

HOW DO YOU RECOGNISE US?

- A word or diagram blurs when we stare at it (this is the quickest way to tell if a kid may be a fast processor).
- We are intelligent — sometimes extraordinarily so — but don't do well in school because simple things like spelling or arithmetic may be difficult or impossible unless they are taught in a way we can grasp and understand.
- We speak quickly, and tend to gabble.
- Spelling and reading are poor, although once reading is learnt we are fast, often fanatical readers.
- We invert words or even swap words in sentences, and sometimes have problems with the letters b and d, p and q, b and p, etc.
- We're good at analysis; we can often make far-flung connections that no one else has thought of.
- We learn best when connections are there to be made, rather than just lists of information.
- We're messy.
- We can not only do two things at once — even carry on two conversations at once — but delight in doing so.
- We try to do *everything*, rushing from one project to the next passion. As a school report said of one child: *George will never regret the things he has never tried to do …*

- We have poor coordination, especially left–right, but it's also bad for dancing, athletics, etc.
- We have problems focusing. I can only read a line of text if I do it *fast*, otherwise it all blurs.

WHAT TO DO

- *Don't* give fast processors the standard reading coaching text — large words and only a few on the page. This makes the problem worse, as the kids can't focus on large words.
- Fast processors need *lots* of text on a page, or comic strips which have few words but lots of images to focus on.
- Don't point to each word as they read. This makes everything much worse for them. They need to be able to see everything at a glance, so trying to slow down their focus makes it almost impossible for them.
- Teach these fast processors touch typing, and then teach them to use the computer. This is possibly the single most important thing you can do for them. Computers go fast, so children with this problem will be able to both read and write fast too. And the faster they can go, the easier it will be for them.

Typing requires a different kind of coordination from that used when you are writing a word with a pencil. Many fast processors find that because they only have to concentrate on one thing at a time — they don't have to focus or form their letters, which are both problems — it's easier to type than write.

- **Teach calligraphy** — writing by hand — only when the kid is a fluent writer on the computer. It's *much* easier to learn

- **Don't bother with spelling** until the kids are confident typists and readers.

- **Give them advanced reading material.**
  It's not easier for these children to read simple texts — in fact it's more difficult, as the words are usually spread out.

- **Try giving them comics** — especially sophisticated *Phantom*-type ones that adults also like. There is a lot of picture activity on each page, even if only a small amount of text.

- **Don't get fast processors to use a computer spellcheck as they work** — it'll just interrupt their flow — but do encourage them to use it afterwards and to do their own editing.

- Once they have mastered writing and reading, give them regular extra coaching if possible to catch up on all the sentence construction, punctuation, etc., that they have missed.

Social learners

These are kids who find their friends more important than schoolwork. They want to fit in, not show anyone up or seem brighter or more able than the rest of the class. They aren't enormously *interested* in excelling. These are usually extremely emotionally talented kids, and will be brilliantly emotionally talented adults.

WHAT TO DO

- **Don't panic and push.** Social learners just want to be *good enough*. And good enough will get them where they want to go. Emotionally talented kids can often judge extremely well just how much they need to achieve to get what they want, like the lowest possible mark to get into their university course. You may want your child to be top of the class.

- **Make reading a social event** and get your child to read with his best friend (a dog can be a best friend, so can a horse or toy wombat). Best friends are often more intuitive teachers too, as they have more experience of a friend's needs and more recent experiences of how they learnt that technique. (I learnt algebra from my best friend in five minutes, after hours of formal teaching had failed.) Ask them to help younger children, encourage them to join or form a club — a horse club, a fan club, anything that involves being social and using their reading and writing.

- **Let kids talk about their lessons in class** (see A Classroom Revolution in Chapter 13). Social learners learn best — or sometimes *only* learn — when they share information with others.

- **Suggest that your child teach the dog/teddy bear/toy stegosaurus/their younger brother what they have learnt at school.** Social learners *love* teaching and helping others, and by teaching others they learn themselves and reinforce their skills.

- **Enrol your child in a 'buddy system' to help younger kids learn.**

- **Ask your child what she has learnt each day and discuss it.** But you won't be able to fake an interest: if you are busy and preoccupied, she'll pick up on it.

- **Suggest writing a small magazine or newsletter** with and for his friends on subjects that interest them — whether it is fashion or fishing, music or motors.

- **Let kids know early on about the caring professions, from social work, medicine, speech therapy and music therapy to teaching.** Convince them that they'll need to do reasonably well at school if they want to get into these important and rewarding areas. Find them books about people helping people or doing things together or about animals.

Active children and kinetic learners

The active child is the one who always seems to be wriggling around. He develops ants in his pants if you try to get him to concentrate on a page (and, yes, he's more often a boy). He would rather be galloping across the plains or conquering the universe than sitting still!

There are many reasons children may seem to be 'hyperactive' — so active that they just can't concentrate on things.

- They may just notice more of what's happening around them — like visual processors — and so be more easily distracted.
- They may be bored in class because what's going on *appears* boring to them.
- They may be fast processors (see page 154).
- They may be being bullied at school and are too stressed to concentrate. Stress can manifest itself as restless, pointless (to the observer) activity, rather like the displacement activity that captive animals sometimes engage in.
- They may be stressed by family or other problems.
- They may have an attention deficit disorder (see page 192).

I suspect that the most common reason why some children, more usually boys, can't sit still long enough to learn is just that they are physical little creatures who like moving about and do not actually have an attention disorder.

WHAT TO DO FOR KIDS WHO NEED REGULAR DEBOUNCING:

- Encourage kids to walk or bicycle to school.
- Get rid of school bells and have dance music instead. Kids — and teachers — have to dance for five minutes before school and before each class.
- Make sure that there are places to play safely, that is, not just asphalt.
- Have a 'library' of balls, cricket bats, skipping ropes, etc., for kids to borrow at lunchtime.
- Have a school vegetable garden and chooks.
- Have trees to climb, and encourage kids to climb them.
- Offer lunchtime and after-school lessons in karate, ballet, dancing, gymnastics, swimming, etc. These are especially important in after-school care. Kids may be mentally tired after school, but physical activity — even just a long walk or an hour in a swimming pool — can refresh them.
- Make sure the school has access to a swimming pool, for hot afternoons.

- Have lessons that involve movement, not just sitting still. See 'kinetic learners' below.

Kinetic learners

Very active children may be kinetic learners — they learn better by *doing* things.

SIGNS OF A KINETIC LEARNER

- They love *doing* things: making, watching, enquiring.
- They wriggle when they have to sit still for long and stop listening, but if you're on a walk they'll ask questions the whole time — and listen to the answers.
- They concentrate better after they've been active for an hour or six.
- They doodle or fiddle when you are talking to them, but still take in what you are saying.
- They are endlessly enquiring about the world as long as they don't need to sit still to do it.
- They are good at multi-tasking: listening to music while talking to you and doing their homework and watching TV.
- They concentrate superbly on what they are interested in, and ignore what they're not interested in.
- They're active. A lot.
- They possibly walked at a younger than usual age, are expert tree climbers, often have unusually

accurate eyesight and other physical skills, from being able to rock-hop up a creek to playing a beat on the kitchen table.

The ideas below are great for *all* kids, not just kinetic learners. Kids are small bundles of energy, and learn better when they are thoroughly debounced but not over-tired. Kids also learn better with many different styles of teaching, not just the 'all sit down and listen and watch' kind.

WHAT TO DO

- **Teach writing while moving.** Find a blank concrete wall outside. Use water pistols to write words. (I bet they'll still be there writing when it's time for bed.)
- **Give kids small water pistols filled with water-based paint,** and have them write words with water pistols on butcher's paper — bathing costumes and an outside venue are a must for this!
- **Play a 'Run and Chant' game.** Make kids run once around the garden or playground chanting the spelling of one word. When they get back they have to write it down. Once they manage that, they get another word and another run.
- **Give kids cardboard with words written on it and some Blu Tack.** They have to move around the house

or school attaching them to the appropriate item and then have to take them off.

- **Make plasticine letters** and then make words with them.
- **Write in sand** — but not enormous letters as then they wouldn't be able to focus on the words. Letters about thirty centimetres high should be big enough to be fun but not too/so large as to cause focusing problems.
- **Write with a torch** while they spell out various words. Get them to jump as they say each letter.
- **Encourage your child to learn good physical crafts** like weaving, cooking, gardening, woodworking, etc. but give them books and articles about it too, so that they learn the theory as well as the practice. This also goes for any sport they love; show them that there is a theoretical as well as a practical side to any sport, with information available on everything from training methods and diet to the lives of sporting heroes.
- **Do a mural or a learning wall** during each school term in the family room. Stick butcher's paper on a wall and every day get your child to add something they've learnt, such as new spelling words, labelled drawings or even just drawings. Add the times-tables, a map of explorers' journeys — whatever's relevant. Writing up what children have learnt is a good way

to really fix the information in their mind — and again they are up and doing something, instead of just sitting and watching TV.

- **Learn touch typing.** Many active children will find touch-typing a wonderful option. They will be able to work *fast*. Show them how to link onto their favourite internet sites too — sport sites, science or movie sites.

- **Try comics,** ones with lots of adventures like *The Phantom* or humour like *Footrot Flats* that they can read quickly for fun and dash off to play again. I wish that all libraries had a stack of comics for children. A comic book can be a great learning aid, to give children fluency and make them realise that reading is actually fun. Each picture in a comic gives the child clues about what the text is about, and the short snappy text is very easy to focus on too. Most children *love* comics, and they can really get reluctant readers going.

    Once they have been beguiled by the short snappy comic-book format move on to the longer story-length comics like the *Asterix* and *Tin Tin* series, loved by so many kids (especially those with a bent towards history or geography).

- **Keep them at it!** Active kids have so much else preoccupying them that they easily forget what they've learnt yesterday: retention of information or skills becomes a problem. So much learning is cumulative and sequential that poor retention can become a quite disabling problem. Regular short sessions every day until they read fluently are essential.

Easily distracted children

It's often difficult to tell whether a child has a genuine reading problem or ADD/ADHD or is just very active. And some children have never learnt to concentrate for any length of time.

WHAT TO DO

If you suspect that your child *does* have ADD or ADHD, ask your family doctor for a referral to a specialist or seek an appointment with an occupational therapist who specialises in children who have concentration problems.

There may be other reasons — emotional or nutritional or some other undiagnosed medical problem. Children who have hearing or sight problems often seem easily distracted because they are unable to see or hear well enough to concentrate.

Ask yourself as well whether your child *really* is easily distracted or just very active. A very active child will concentrate for extended periods on the things that interest her. An easily distracted child finds it difficult to settle on anything for long.

If your child is just an active child, go with the flow! Count your blessings that she is energetic and healthy and may also be extremely bright. A real passion for getting into things and inquisitiveness are often signs of high intelligence.

HOW TO TEACH KIDS TO CONCENTRATE

Concentration needs to be learnt. Some kids learn it themselves. Other kids need intensive teaching.

- **Turn off the TV** and try to provide your child with quiet spaces and quiet times.
- **Set a good example** by giving yourself some quiet time too. If you're always flustered and jumping from one disaster to another, your child will learn to do the same.
- Show them organisation and organisational techniques:
  - make lists of things to be done — and let them see that you also have lists of things to help you keep your life in order
  - have a schedule for each day of the week on a whiteboard in their room or in the kitchen
  - sort clothes into categories
  - sort rubbish for recycling and place it in the correct bins.
- Teach children how to focus for longer and longer periods by:

- reading them long, complex but fascinating stories, like *Harry Potter* or *Lord of the Rings*
- telling them long, involved and interesting stories about when you or their grandparents were young so that they get used to listening for longer periods of time
- turning off the TV at mealtimes and having long conversations instead: they will learn that one remark can lead to another and then to a discussion where they have to think and put their thoughts in order and into the best words possible.

- **Teach kids to think, focus and argue** by discussing social, political and moral issues with them.
- **Ban yelling.** Kids yell when they don't know how to put the case for what they want. 'I want it *now*! Everyone else has one!' is not an argument, it's a demand. An argument is a reasoned discussion, and it doesn't have to get heated, although it may if people feel passionate about a position. (It's important for children to know that they can put a case and be heard and also that other people can state their position and some things will remain unresolved to be thought about and returned to later.) But children do need to practise thinking things out; help them to get their thoughts out into the open.

- **Encourage long projects** or craftwork that will take several sessions to complete (or make real progress!). Let kids choose something they are interested in. Take them to the non-fiction section of the library and fossick around for good suggestions. This teaches kids that the more work you put into something, the more fascinating it becomes.

- **Teach children how to work on lengthy tasks** — how to plan what they are going to do, get the right materials, do the job, finish the job and clean up afterwards (and this usually involves more list-making with subsidiary lists as well). A good practice job is repainting garden furniture or the garden fence. Let them choose the colours. A friend and her children wallpapered their toilet with two-hundred pages filled with children's drawings, poems, jokes, times-tables and favourite pictures cut out from magazines. It took most of one set of school holidays and each summer holiday to re-do it. It is the most fascinating loo I know.

HOW TO IMPROVE MEMORY AND RECALL

Children also need to develop the ability to recall and remember things. And again, some children are slower at acquiring these skills than others. And, yes, like many other skill sets, memory can be taught and developed. There are a number of strategies you can use to teach children how to remember.

REPEATING WHAT THEY ARE TOLD

Mum: Go and get your raincoat. Now, what did I ask you to do?

Jason: Go and get my raincoat.

Mum: OK, now think it inside your head instead of saying it. Can you do that?

Jason: (Nods.)

Mum: Good boy!

IMAGINING WHAT THEY ARE TOLD

Dad: If I have to remember something, I try to imagine it in my head. If Mum says, 'Will you put out the clothes, please?' I make a picture in my mind of me carrying the clothes basket. How about you try it? If I say, 'Get your raincoat, please?' what will you do?

Jason: Imagine me fetching my raincoat.

Dad: That's good! Now, are you doing that?

Jason: (Nods.)

MEMORY GAMES

I Packed My Bag and I Took …

Each person in turn has to add an imaginary item to an imaginary bag and remember all the other items added by other family members.

Dad: I packed my bag and I took a banana.

Mum: I packed my bag and I took a banana and an apple.

Emma: I packed my bag and I took a banana and an apple and a fruit popper!

And so on!

This is a great game to help teach children how to remember things, especially if you say: 'Imagine each one in the bag,' or 'Try to link each one in some way: a banana is bigger than an apple and an apple is smaller than a fruit popper ...'. It's also a good game for in the car — opportunities for fun and laughter as well as building up an efficient and useful memory.

Slow learners

These children aren't just slow at learning to read and write. They are slower to learn all sorts of things.

The emphasis here, however, is on slow*er*. These children will learn to read, write and whatever else they need to learn, but it will take them more time — and if that time isn't given to them right at the beginning, they will get further and further behind. With these children it's not so much a matter of how to teach them — it's finding the extra time and human resources to do it. And they will keep learning all their life.

Adults often severely underestimate children who are slow learners. I remember my first public reading of one of my stories. The third group to come in were children with an intellectual disability and I thought, Hey, this is impossible, I wrote this story for extra bright children!

I've never had such a wonderful audience. I had to speak much more slowly, it's true, and keep pausing. But they laughed in all the right places and at one point, when a child in the story says that adults often agree with you because they don't really listen to you, some of the audience literally fell off their seats laughing and gave pointed looks towards their carers.

These children were slow learners — but they understood everything the other children did, and more. Give these children time and they'll get there.

WHAT TO DO
Slow learners often benefit from some of the suggestions for very active children too, as their attention span may be limited.

But mostly reassure slow learners that they *will* get there in the end.

A friend's daughter with severe intellectual impairment is nearly forty. In the past year her reading has improved enough for her to be able to sort mail in an office. Luckily she's in a loving and supportive group house with a loving and supportive family, because she'll continue to learn all her life. (We all do.)

Never think a child can't learn. But it does take some kids — and adults — longer. Even much longer.

The worst thing you can do for a child is convince him that he is stupid and that there is no hope.

On that note, we once had a man classified as having an intellectual disability work on our property for a fortnight. Yes, he was slow at understanding things and he was a very slow reader. But he was also fascinated by the wildlife here and — slowly — made his way through a heap of CSIRO scientific reports on wallabies, platypus and habitat destruction.

Above all, do give slow learners good and challenging books once they *do* learn to read, and in the meantime read to them — their favourite books and books about things that interest them.

Slow language developers

These are usually boys — and sometimes boys with a loving older sibling or caring parent who makes it easy for them to live comfortably without talking much. (If you ever hear one of your children — or yourself — say, 'Little Bernard would love a slice of cake, please,' instead of letting little Bernard ask himself, take a closer look at little Bernard's language development in case he has problems that you — with the best will in the world — have been perpetuating. This is quite easy to correct — the tougher task is when an older sibling, often a sister, takes over interpreting the world for a younger child and interpreting that child to the world.)

Children who are slow at learning and using language will probably be slower at learning to read.

They may also have problems learning to hear the sounds that make up individual words.

HOW TO TELL IF A CHILD IS A SLOW LANGUAGE DEVELOPER

- They are slower to learn individual words than other children their age.
- They are slower to speak in sentences.
- They're not having conversations (that is using full sentences with the words placed in appropriate semantic order rather than a series of disjointed words accompanied by pointing and gestures) by the time they are three.
- They play silently with other children or, more likely, have a range of noises — the roar of a truck, the whir of a flying plane — that they use instead.
- They let the other child 'tell the story' of the game they are playing, while they concentrate on the action.

On the other hand, they are no slower at learning to walk, catch balls, play happily with children their own age or a bit older or understand what's going on around them. They are generally as bright as — or even much brighter than — most children.

Some people – kids and adults – prefer listening to talking. If one of your son's parents or grandparents is on the quiet side too, then the chances are that you have a quiet, thoughtful child. Only worry if you think your child isn't understanding language, as well as not wanting to talk much.

WHAT TO DO

- **Be patient and don't panic.** Yes, learning to speak early and using enough words to stump a professor of English *is* a sign of high intelligence, but a child can be a slow language developer and still be brilliant. They are slower, but they will catch up and even overtake their peers in language ability.
- Seek help the minute you suspect that your child is taking longer than other children to talk fluently. Take your child to a speech therapist. OK, she may just be slow, but there may also be another problem that needs treating. The speech therapist can also help your child catch up with her peers.
- **Say words very, very clearly** when children are learning to read. They may be slower at learning to pick out individual sounds. And try to speak clearly and distinctly as much as you can without going totally barmy with the effort.
- **Play Making Word Sounds** from Chapter 1 regularly — in the car or walking to school.
- Help your child through each stage of learning to read with the techniques outlined in Chapter 4.

Ask for advice from your child's teacher and learning support teacher.

MABEL'S STORY

I came across Mabel a couple of years ago. She had no particular education herself — left school at twelve, married at seventeen — but for years she had been volunteering at the local school to help children with reading problems — and she had the most extraordinary success rate. People spoke of her as though she had magic in her fingertips.

Her secret? Mabel had a naturally clear, distinct voice and she spoke slowly and deliberately. All those children who were having problems simply hearing how words were made up had no problems at all when they tried to write or read the words Mabel articulated. And she had enormous patience, tolerance and love — the children felt cherished rather than shoved into a group of dummies. Sometimes you just get a miracle like Mabel.

P.S. I suspect that after thirty years Mabel also had the experience to know when to suggest a visit to the doctor or other specialist.

Bright but bored children

These kids are often misdiagnosed with ADD or ADHD, though instead of finding it difficult to concentrate, they concentrate extremely well and so have often finished their work long before other children, or they are too bored to begin in the first place. They stare out the window or daydream, if you're lucky, and disrupt the class if you're not.

HOW TO TELL IF A KID IS BRIGHT BUT BORED

- They walk or talk earlier than their peers. Many gifted children don't do this. (One extremely bright young man I know didn't talk until he was three.) But early verbal ability especially is often a sign of a gifted child.
- Do they ask so many questions that you feel like hiding under the bed to get some peace?
- Do they seem to learn things faster than other children their age?
- Are they creative — make up stories, songs, music, drawings, plays (for siblings, other children or even pets and toys to act out) that show originality?
- Are they forever curious and enthusiastic?
- Are they always into things?
- Do they have a memory like an elephant?
- Are they intuitive — able to think and analyse on many levels, rather than just going from A to B? Children who just seem to pluck questions or answers out of thin air are really taking in all sorts of information and decoding and interpreting. (My

step-grandson, for example, asked me how bees made honey. After the explanation, he asked, 'But how do they make the jars?' He was taking what he had been told and adding to it what he knew already: he went one step further.)

- Do they have a wide range of interests? (Leonardo da Vinci was interested in just about every aspect of art and science.) Gifted people are usually fascinated by more than one area and often these interests appear far apart — music and mathematics, for example, which use the same part of the brain, so an affinity with one often means an affinity with the other, or bushwalking and engineering. An early and intense interest in lots of things is a sign of a gifted child.

WHAT TO DO

Kids who poke their fingers into sofas, who ask one hundred and forty-six questions before breakfast, who always want to *do* things and need at least four adults to keep them amused and occupied can give a saint a breakdown in twenty minutes. But all these are also signs of highly intelligent children who process information quickly and are hungry for more.

The sooner these children learn to read and find the books they enjoy and need, or learn how to manipulate computers, circuit boards or any other activity that they'll finding challenging and absorbing and open-ended (the more they do, the more they'll find *to* do) the better for everyone's sanity.

You may think that a gifted child will never have a reading problem, but this isn't the case. Sometimes these children are just so bored that they don't pay any attention at all.

Gifted children may also be fast processors and have great trouble doing things slowly. Even if your child isn't a fast processor, many of the hints given earlier for those children will be useful for a gifted child.

Children who have just missed out

This is possibly the most common reason why children have reading problems; they have missed out on a step or two somewhere either because they were away from school or were stressed about something for a while or had a teacher that they didn't get on with or a disruptive child sitting next to them or a family that kept moving from one region to another and they miss out on vital chunks of information in the process. A friend who volunteers with the MultiLit program had one little girl in year three who had in four short years been taught in schools in Tasmania, Victoria, the ACT, NSW, back to Tasmania, Queensland and back to NSW. She just kept getting further and further behind.

These children don't need an underlying problem solved; they just need a bit of help to get them on the right track.

WHAT TO DO

- Ask the school what learning support they offer. If they don't offer any, have a very public tantrum till they do, if you can do this without embarrassing the kid who needs it. Or organise it yourself — whatever works.
- Go through the reading steps in Chapter 3 to see where the problem is and then work on that area at home. Tell the teacher where your child is having problems so that he or she can help them catch up.

Physical problems that interfere with reading: and how to help

Children with reading problems *may* need a specialised diagnosis by one of the following specialists:

- an ophthalmologist who specialises in reading problems
- an audiologist
- a speech therapist
- an occupational therapist
- a nutritionist
- a neurologist
- an educational psychologist

- a psychiatrist
- a consultative paediatrician who can assess any sleep or other health problems.

Some children may need to see more than one of these; others may not need to see any. But many reading difficulties *will* need an expert diagnosis and, in other cases, rare and dangerous conditions such as brain tumours still need to be ruled out.

WHAT TO DO IF YOU THINK YOUR CHILD MAY HAVE A PHYSICAL PROBLEM

Consult a paediatrician

Sometimes medical problems make it difficult for children to learn. They could have anything from a gluten allergy to a snoring problem. You will probably suspect that something is wrong already, if it is a health problem rather than a learning one, but if you are concerned ask your GP for a referral to a paediatrician.

Consult an educational psychologist

An educational psychologist can assess a child's intellectual function and educational attainment, and obtain an overview of their auditory and visual skills. A psychologist's report will also be necessary for older children if they need to ask for extra time for examinations (and other allowances in years ten and twelve), and it may also help in convincing the school to let the child use a laptop in class, or to provide other assistance such as a special-education teacher to work with him.

Not all psychologists will continue to work with your child. Most will just give you an assessment of whether there is a problem or not. Some may refer you to other specialists who can design a program of assistance; others may leave this up to you. In other words, a psychologist may be able to tell you if there is a problem, but may not be able to offer solutions. This varies from psychologist to psychologist and some do specialise in learning difficulties and will be able to give a lot more help.

If you can't find/afford an educational psychologist, the list and techniques following may help diagnose the problem.

Consult the class teacher

Teachers see children with others of their age and can often judge whether a child has problems, or is just young for her age. This can be a delicate balancing act for teachers — many parents become offended when a teacher says that their child has a learning difficulty.

It is possible that your child may just be having problems in one area of learning and the teacher can give her extra work to do at home so that she can catch up. The teacher can also refer the child to the school's special-education teacher (assuming the school has one).

Consult the special-education teacher

A special-education teacher may be able to recognise a child with special needs and coordinate the appropriate referral. They should be familiar with specialists who liaise with the school and work with other professionals to provide appropriate support for your child at school.

All being well, the special-education teacher will work out which specialist the child needs, liaise with the specialist and parents to help coordinate any treatment, and help the child catch up with his schoolwork.

If the school does not have a special-education teacher, ask your family doctor for a recommendation or contact SPELD (an organisation devoted to helping people with Specific Learning Difficulties). This organisation can provide specialist advice in an enormous range of areas, including the recommendation of psychologists and specialist tutors, computer programs, reading material and specialist programs to help literacy, for example, MultiLit. Look in the phone book or on the internet for your local branch.

Act!

If the teacher can't help, and there is no specialist help offered by the school, it's up to you. The gut feelings of parents are pretty reliable. If you suspect a serious problem, be persistent! Your family doctor or your child's teacher may well be reassuring, and say, 'They'll grow out of it' or that 'They are within normal range for their age' or 'Let's just wait and see'. Trust your instincts! Get specialist help *now*. The longer problems are left the harder it is for children to catch up, and the bigger the scars they'll have from thinking they are dumb.

Be prepared to try many specialists. Sometimes children may need more than one. But it can be worth it: a few months with the right specialist can make it seem as though a miracle has occurred.

Visual problems

Eyesight and focusing problems are possibly some of the most commonly misdiagnosed causes of reading problems.

Some children have problems seeing words and letters or making sense of what they see. This can be simple long-sightedness, easily treated and diagnosed and treated by an optometrist, but there are other ocular conditions that limit a child's ability to focus on or make sense of what they see — these must be diagnosed by an ophthalmologist who specialises in these problems.

Some children have problems reading in certain lighting conditions or can focus better wearing prescribed coloured lenses.

If your child turns their head as they read a page or often loses her place, she may have problems coordinating her eye movements.

If your child can only see a few letters at a time, he may have a small visual span. He has to keep looking back to check what letters he's read.

Some children have problems focusing for longer than a few seconds. After that things blur. (These children will probably hate it if you point to words as you read.)

Some children can see well but can't process what they've seen — they find it difficult to distinguish between shapes or colours, or can't remember what they've seen. This is partly inherited and partly learnt. All children have to learn how to remember what they've seen and put the pieces together to make sense of it — for example, they put together mouth, nose and eyes and say, 'Hey, that's Mum!'

Early clues that your child may have a visual problem:

- If your preschool child isn't as good as other children at making things out of blocks or Lego or joining the dots.

- If your older child keeps misreading words like *cat* for *cut* or leaves the ends off words or misreads 69 for 96.

WHAT TO DO

- Ask your GP for a referral to an optometrist or ophthalmologist who specialises in developmental problems.
- An optometrist will check your child's eyesight and recommend glasses if necessary. You don't need a doctor's referral to go to an optometrist — you'll find a list of them in the phone book or on the internet. But your child may not need glasses; she may have other problems that can be diagnosed by a behavioural optometrist.
- A behavioural optometrist will investigate what your child's eyes do. Children with reading difficulties often have problems with convergence and tracking, and the behavioural optometrist can discover if this is the case, and will also give you ways to overcome the problem.

     Don't think that because a general optometrist has checked your child's eyes and says he is not short- or long-sighted that he is necessarily OK. The optometrist needs to be experienced in visual perception tests and visual motor coordination tests (although they may use different names for these) and be able to give you a report on what the problems are and how they can be eased or solved.

You may find that the optometrist works with an occupational therapist, or refers clients to one for help correcting their problems. Children don't have to be long- or short-sighted to have visual problems.

- Have your child taught touch typing. That way she won't have to focus on what she is writing and, as she types, she will become familiar with words and find reading easier.

- Help teach your children to learn how to focus and use their visual memory. As with any skill, the more you do it the better you get — and the earlier you become skilled the better.

- Ask him to practise 'seeing' what he did yesterday. Then ask him where they were or what Fenella was wearing or what flavour his ice cream was.

- Play memory games.

Put an object on the table — say an apple — then ask your child to shut his eyes and remember what it is. When he opens his eyes again, you put a banana next to the apple, and ask him to shut his eyes and say 'a banana and an apple'.

Put twenty things on the table and give the child a minute to look at them. Then they shut their eyes and remember as many things as they can. You should participate in these games too, to show that they're fun, not lessons.

This Way Round: On squares of cardboard draw people (or horses, fish, dogs, etc.) looking to the left. Then draw one person or animal looking to the right. Your child has to choose which one is looking to the right.

Or play card games like Snap or Old Maid or play dominoes.

Hearing problems

Many children have trouble hearing at some stage because of wax or water in their ears or after a cold or other illness. While this is temporary, it can still interfere with learning to speak and use words. Other children may lose some of their ability to hear from illness, or it may be inherited.

Many newborn babies are now tested for hearing, and hearing deficits can be picked up in the first few days of life. Children as young as two months can be tested for deafness. But even if an issue is missed at these checks, as a child gets older, you can pick up clues. If you suspect that your child has hearing problems, talk to your doctor at once. Early diagnosis and treatment as well as learning support will make an enormous difference.

DEAFNESS CLUES

Does your child:

- watch your face carefully when you are talking to them, or turn their head to one side?
- have trouble talking or understanding when the TV is on?
- confuse the beginning or ends of words?
- not like playing with children not familiar to them? (Bear in mind that the reasons for this may be many and varied.)

Some children are not really deaf but do have some trouble isolating the sounds that they want to hear (or that you want them to hear) from competing sounds.

WORD DISCRIMINATION PROBLEMS

Does your child:

- confuse similar sounding words like *pat* and *pot* or *big* and *bag*?
- have problems with rhyming words?
- mispronounce *lots* of words?

WHAT TO DO

Some children are just slower than others at learning to discriminate between sounds. It doesn't mean that they lack intelligence or are slow generally — they're just slower in that area of learning. Others may have a hearing problem.

- Ask your family doctor for a referral to an ear, nose and throat specialist, and an audiologist.
- Even if your child doesn't have a hearing problem, make sure that you speak clearly and distinctly to your children. *Turn off the tv and radio (and other sources of sound such as music and computer games etc) as much as possible.* It is difficult for a child to learn how words are pronounced if there are other human voices in the background. Make sure you talk to your child for at least an hour a day in a quiet spot with no other human voices.
- Ask other members of the family (and this includes adults) not to play computer games while the child is attempting to read or listen, learning to spell or taking a dictation.

WHO TO CONSULT FOR HELP

An audiologist

Audiologists check to see that the child can hear. Some audiologists have additional specialist training in following what the brain does with what it hears. They can check for auditory processing disorders.

A speech and language pathologist

These specialists will investigate your child's strengths and weaknesses when using language. They'll be able to work out a program to help improve skills like visual sequencing, memory and sound awareness.

They'll also give ongoing therapy (tutoring) and counselling. Most speech and language pathologists work in close connection with schools and other professionals.

HOW TO HELP YOUR CHILD DISCRIMINATE BETWEEN SOUNDS

Discriminating between sounds is also a learnt skill — one that can be taught. Take time to listen to different sounds with your child. The following are some useful games you can play with your child. None of these strategies will be an instant solution — but slowly and surely they will make a great difference.

SITTING AND LISTENING

You can play this game in the car, at the beach, anywhere that there are different sounds to listen to.

Mum: What can you hear, Emma?

Emma: (Shrugs.)

Mum: I can hear a car. What sound does a car make, Emma?

Emma: Vroom!

Mum: Can you hear a truck too? It's a different sound. Can you hear it?

RHYMING GAMES

Adults should take the initiative with this game, but later children will probably choose to join in.

Dad: I see a car. Ha, ha, ha, I see a car. I see a dog, no it's not a frog, it's a dog, dog, dog. I see a cat; it's very fat.

You don't have to do this so often that you sound demented, just now and then. Children like rhymes and rhyme games and will work hard at joining in. You can also try making up sentences using as many words that start with the same sound as possible: *King Cat caught a carrot.* When children can make up sentences like this themselves, try finding words that end in the same sound: runn*ing*, jump*ing*, fish*ing*; b*at*, f*at*, c*at*, m*at*, s*at*.

COPYING 'FACE SOUNDS'

You go 'oo' and exaggerate the shape your lips make to produce the sound. Then have your child make the same sound, moving their lips in the same way. Do a few new sounds every day.

Attention disorders

Attention Deficit Disorder (ADD) and Attention Deficit Hyperactive Disorder (ADHD) do exist. Yes, some children are wrongly diagnosed as having ADD, but others are dramatically helped by either the medication or learning support specifically tailored for ADD/ADHD children.

The trouble is that you can't take a blood test and discover that a child has ADD/ADHD. Doctors diagnose the disorders because of the way the children behave — they're impulsive, inattentive or hyperactive, with poor short-term memories. There can be many other reasons why the child has all of those symptoms: they may be very bright and very bored; they may be a naturally active child; they may be so deeply upset by a school or home problem that they can't concentrate; or they may have a hearing, visual or some other problem which diminishes their concentration skills.

Not all ADD children are hyperactive, although they're the ones that you mostly notice. Some ADD children can be quiet and withdrawn and daydream a lot, but still have poor short-term memory, be impulsive and have difficulty concentrating. Other children can learn to concentrate with the help of an occupational therapist — and for these children medication is not the long-term solution.

Doctors and, to some extent, counsellors and teachers only see children under a limited range of conditions. Parents, however, need to work out if their child has problems under *all* situations. For example, if a child is just having trouble concentrating at school, it may be that she is bored, or being bullied, or has a specific learning difficulty. If the child is bright it may mean that she is bored and so will fidget or be disruptive.

SIGNS THERE MAY BE A PROBLEM

- Does your child act first and think later? (Of course he does. He's a kid!) But does he do it more than other children his age?
- Does your child have trouble remembering that you asked her to get her jumper two minutes ago? (Yes, of course she does if preoccupied by cartoons or a mate's visit. But again does she do it more than other children her age?)
- Does your child have problems concentrating? This is really the key question. Very active children may seem to have problems concentrating because they'd rather be out doing things! But when they are doing things — painting the garden furniture twenty-seven colours, playing a sport that needs concentration, building the most magnificent sandcastle on the beach — they can concentrate wonderfully (children with Asperger's syndrome do this).

Children with other learning difficulties may not be able to concentrate enough to read, but they will concentrate for so long on a complex story that's being read to them that the reader loses her voice.

Children with ADD/ADHD have concentration and memory problems in *most* situations — not just some of them.

WHAT TO DO

- Have your child diagnosed by a doctor who specialises in this area. Provide the doctor with as much information as you can to help their diagnosis, but try to be even-handed — academic parents who have a child who would rather be zipping around a football field than reading and who loves comic books instead of *The Wind in the Willows* can so easily think their child has a problem. She doesn't — she's just different from you.

- Work out a wide-ranging treatment regime with the doctor — not just medication. Children with ADD/ADHD will need help with learning skills like organisation and concentration; even if the medication is successful, it won't solve all the problems. Medication alone is never enough.

- AND — as well as seeing a doctor, consult an occupational therapist. You may find that your child just needs professional help to learn to concentrate.

- A child with ADD/ADHD may also need to be assessed and treated for hearing or visual problems — speech therapy and occupational therapy may help here too.

- And both children and parents may find counselling helps them cope with the problems that having ADD/ADHD (and having a child with ADD/ADHD) can cause.

- Follow the exercises on page 167: How to teach kids to concentrate.
- Check the information on fast processors on pages 154. These children are sometimes misdiagnosed as ADD/ADHD. They concentrate so well that they need to zap through things to find more stimulation and they can be bored with children their age and therefore don't mix well. But these children do concentrate well at home. This is where the assessment of a child by both parents *and* teachers is crucial — the parents know what the child is like when he is happy and interested, the teachers know how well he is performing compared to other children.

Coordination problems

Is your child clumsy? Unable to coordinate her writing, catch balls or ride a bicycle?

There can be many reasons for coordination problems, from eyesight problems to brain injury, at birth or acquired, muscular dystrophy, motor neurone disease, epilepsy, multiple sclerosis, brain tumours, thyroid problems, diabetes or hyperglycaemia. All of these will have other symptoms too, but it is worth having any coordination problem checked out by a professional.

WHAT TO DO

Have a chat with your family doctor

Make a list of all possible symptoms before your visit — often one symptom alone may not strike a chord, but several together will suggest what the problem may be. Your doctor may refer you to other specialists for further tests. Do not panic; they'll usually be ruling out severe but very unlikely causes.

Consult an occupational therapist

Occupational therapists assess and work with children who have coordination, concentration, handwriting or other sensory problems. Sometimes children diagnosed with Attention Deficit Disorder (ADD/ADHD) have never learnt how to concentrate, and can be taught.

Encourage your child to play a sport or do an activity that teaches coordination

Karate is excellent, with repeated left–right exercises with hands and feet. It also has no obvious connection with reading problems, so kids won't be embarrassed doing it. I've seen clumsy teenagers blossom and no longer worry exactly where to put their hands and feet after they have been exposed to a few months of jazz ballet or gymnastics. Ballet, dancing, ice-skating, swimming, any ball game, competitive Frisbee throwing, tai chi and many other activities all teach hand–eye coordination and how to use and move your body, as well as being fun and keeping children fit.

Teach your child ball-against-the-wall games, jacks or knuckles, skipping games, juggling, stilt-walking and other circus skills. All these are wonderful approaches for developing different levels of fine and gross motor coordination.

As above, show your child how to touch type. Don't worry, she *will* learn handwriting, because children like to be like everyone else.

MAJOR COORDINATION PROBLEMS

If your child has a permanent or temporary problem that won't allow him to use an ordinary computer, he needs a keyboard made especially for him. An occupational therapist and their medical team should be able to arrange this but if not, or if it's too expensive, charities like Variety or your local Rotary or Lodge of Truth or CWA or church may help you raise funds for it. They are also good places to ask for help with wheelchairs specially designed for kids to play sport or dance.

Mostly, remember there are many people who *do* want to help. By asking you are giving them the chance to do what humans feel best about: helping others. Especially kids.

Eating problems

Is your child eating well enough, or could she be diabetic or hyperglycaemic? As any parent who's been to a child's birthday party knows, sugar highs exist. Some children who eat junk food, especially lots of sweet food with no protein or complex carbohydrates to balance it, may well have problems concentrating. There have also been studies that imply that regularly eating oily fish, or taking fish oil, may improve learning problems. This is still a long way from being proved, but fish is low in fat and a good source of protein so there are other reasons to add it to a kid's diet.

Children who are diabetic or hyperglycaemic may also have problems concentrating.

WHAT TO DO

If your family has a history of diabetes or hyperglycaemia and you suspect that your child has problems, ask your family doctor to give him a glucose tolerance test. And if you are unsure what your child should be eating for his best development — or have a child who is a picky eater, who demands junk food or has developed other bad eating habits — ask your doctor for a referral to a nutritionist. They'll not only be able to say what your child should be eating, they'll help with strategies to make sure he does.

Food can often become a power battle between parent and child. If your child has a limited range of things she will eat, start working on the problem. (A few cookbooks with bright pictures of healthy foods are a great start — get your children to participate in choosing and cooking the recipe you'll cook next.)

The medical exceptions to this common-sense approach are anorexia (which needs immediate diagnosis and treatment if you suspect it) and bulimia (literally starving and gorging, it also needs professional help at once).

Vegetarianism, which is a legitimate moral stand that children may decide to make (it may also be a way of asserting their individuality — but that isn't a bad thing either), is however no excuse for not eating well. The family cooks may just have to discover a few more sources of protein and iron, and there are plenty of books that give advice. Hunt them down in the local library.

Too often, children hate eating fruit and vegetables because no one has ever tried to make them attractive. Many children are intimidated by a whole large apple, but will eat a plate of sliced fruit.

Kids who eat breakfast do better during the day than kids who do not eat breakfast. Kids who have eaten a low-GI breakfast — one that slowly and steadily releases its energy — work better than those

who eat a sugar- and processed grain-rich cereal,
pancakes or toast. Protein (eggs, nuts, lentils, beans,
fish) and dairy (milk, cheese, yoghurt) plus a low-GI
grain food like oatmeal porridge or multigrain bread,
or pancakes made with multigrain flour, or a toasted
cheese sandwich on multigrain bread, will give kids a
head start to their day and their learning.

WHO CAN HELP?

- A paediatric psychologist who specialises in eating
  problems.
- A dietician or nutritionist, if the problem is not
  knowing what is best to eat, rather than an eating
  disorder.
- A support group ... ask your GP for contacts.

Lack of sleep

While this is mostly a problem for adults, children can
have sleep problems too and a lack of sleep will mean
that the child can't pay attention properly at school.

WHAT TO DO

- If your child wakes often during the night, snores,
  coughs, is extremely restless or just doesn't sleep a
  regular nine hours, have a chat with your family
  doctor, who may refer you to a sleep clinic, or an
  ear, nose and throat specialist.

- Have a regular bedtime — and stick to it — and a regular time to get up.
- Make sure that your child has a quiet place to sleep, a comfy bed and a dark room. If necessary, provide earplugs, block-out curtains or a sleeping mask.
- Sometimes, if home life is going to be disrupted at night, it's worth having your child sleep at someone else's house: he goes there when ready for bed, but spends the rest of the time at home. This only works though if there is a place he can go nearby, where he feels safe and comfortable. Some communities with high unemployment, where there may be older brothers and/or sisters who stay up late at night, have created 'sleep houses' where kids can go just to sleep. One child in the Northern Territory, in an area with a truancy rate of over 40%, suggested that school shouldn't start till 4 pm, so he could sleep in till 10 am, and then 'do all the fun stuff'. He says that if school provided a good afternoon tea he and his friends would really enjoy sitting and learning ... but not if he has to get there by 9 am.

Pain

Especially toothache (and chronic earache can be dreadful too): dental care is too expensive for many families and young kids may be left with poor 'first' teeth on the assumption that they will fall out anyway so why waste money getting a filling? If you think a child needs dental or medical help and you can't afford it, ask a local charity to help.

Family issues, stress and worries

It's difficult to concentrate on anything — let alone something as new and complex as learning to read — if you're stressed or worried.

Sometimes children can seem quite happy with changes at home — a new brother or sister, a parent now living away from home, the illness of someone she loves, a grandparent moving in — but her schoolwork is suddenly affected.

WHAT TO DO

- Have patience and don't stress about his temporary slowness. If the problem is temporary then he'll catch up. Concentrate on being loving and reassuring: let him talk; and give him lots of cuddles and a reliably regular routine.
- If problems look like continuing for a while, arrange for her to talk to a counsellor, either a private one or the school counsellor. It's often a good idea to have a chat with the school counsellor anyway if there are problems at home, just so he or she can alert the teachers to be especially tolerant and supportive.

- Encourage children to talk to trustworthy friends and relatives.
- Find the child a mentor figure outside the immediate family, not necessarily to help with his problems, but to give him encouragement and a feeling that he is appreciated. The mentor can be a relative or anyone of standing in the community (from a football coach to a writer) who is prepared to spend time with the child or even write to him regularly and reassure him that he is worthwhile.
- Encourage your child to write about her problems in a diary, or write stories and essays or draw, sculpt or paint. These are all good ways to express pain and distress and put them into a form that doesn't hurt so much.
- Provide refuges in the form of books or DVDs. Make sure that it is happy, relaxing, escapist stuff — because children do need to escape!
- Encourage your child to join a relaxation exercise class or do yoga or meditation or take up power-walking or aerobics for a natural high and also to help him sleep soundly — anything from exhausting exercise to bushwalking and dancing.
- And as for the reading problems, try the steps to reading given in Chapter 4. But don't pressure her. Offer help, but tell her she's wonderful too!

Help from a Psychologist or Psychiatrist

Some children have overwhelming emotional issues that need to be resolved. Others may be suffering from depression or panic attacks. You will need a referral from a doctor for a paediatric psychiatrist or psychologist — one who specialises in children's problems. Ask your doctor's advice. You could also ask the special-education teacher or a paediatrician — anyone regularly involved with children with problems — to recommend a psychiatrist who relates well to kids.

It's important to make sure that the psychiatrist is experienced working with children and their problems, relates well to your child (in particular) and to everyone else involved in helping him. If that isn't happening, go to another.

Psychiatrists do specialise in various problems — and you will probably need one with real experience in this area. But sometimes, too, one with no particular focus on children's problems can develop a great working relationship with a child — be prepared to try another if the first one is unsuccessful.

WHEN I'M STRESSED ...
- I talk about it with family or friends. (Even one conversation can be magic.)

- I go for a walk in the bush — or at least somewhere with trees or water.
- I imagine a wombat munching in our garden (especially when I'm at the dentist) or that I'm floating almost under the water in our swimming hole.
- I imagine I have a monkey's tail that's growing from the end of my spine down, down to the ground then through the earth until it curls around the centre of the planet — that's a good one just before I have to speak in front of an audience.
- I lie on the grass at night and look at a star, and keep watching it move across the sky, slowly feeling the earth below me spin across the universe.
- I put myself on a strict regime of light, funny books and DVDs — especially books that I deeply love. Nothing that will bring tears or make me think, just familiar and happy words.
- I get to work solving the problem. Activity is much less stressful than doing nothing and worrying. Even if I'm just as far from a solution, actually doing something makes me feel better.

Noise and disruption at home

Sometimes, even with the best intentions in the world, home is going to be chaotic, especially if both parents are working or a member of the family is ill or there are long-term visitors or lots of children or ... You can probably add a hundred more things.

WHAT TO DO

- Make a 'quiet place' where children can read, even if it's just a curtained-off spot in the living room or shared bedroom.

  If possible, make this a room where children can read or do homework without any distractions and interruptions from the TV or other children. (I used to read in our family dunny — it was the only quiet place around! Then I made myself a 'room' under the back stairs with a curtain made from an old sheet.)

  Sometimes a parent's bedroom can be designated 'the quiet room' for reading or studying. If this isn't possible, at least give children a quiet corner — and provide earplugs! (They cost a few dollars at the chemist). I'm serious — children are often expected to read or do homework in conditions I couldn't work in!

  And please, please, please, please — turn off the TV! Constant background noise makes it harder to think, work and concentrate.

- Arrange holidays at a friend's or relative's, so kids can relax away from the stress, just for a while. Even a weekend away can help a lot, especially if kids later know that they have a refuge there if things get too bad.

- Talk to your child's teacher and school counsellor, so they know a bit about what your child has to cope with.
- Allow your child time to 'turn off' and read quietly without other demands from family, friends or other organised activities. Stressful times are also times when you need to be quiet and just regroup.
- Give your child half an hour's 'downtime' to read in bed or at least look at pictures in a comic book.
- Arrange a peaceful 'outside' activity once a week. Let your child choose what it is, for example, bushwalking, swimming, dancing.

Stress at school

If a child hates school she probably won't learn well there.

Bullying is, sadly, the most common school problem. However, there can be other problems: the (luckily rare) teacher who takes out his or her own grievances on the children; a 'best friend' who has home problems that are making his or her friends worry too; the child who has become involved with a crowd of children with their own problems and who rebel at learning anything or being cooperative. Sometimes children just feel that they've been in trouble too many times and now feel that they have been labelled a 'troublemaker' and always will be.

Sometimes one child or a small group of disruptive children can disturb the learning of the whole class.

Unfortunately a growing problem in city schools is noise — I was at a (very expensive private) school not long ago where teaching had to be halted every seven minutes as an aircraft flew over. Other schools can be disrupted by traffic or building noise.

For some children a less formal style of teaching and learning can also be a problem; noise and movement around them are extraordinarily disruptive. These children can be helped immensely if you can find a rather traditional school where the children are fairly quiet and remain seated, and there is only one activity going on in the classroom at any one time.

Some children — and adults — can tolerate noisy places. Others find it incredibly difficult to concentrate. (I'm one — I become stressed if there is any loud noise at all around me.)

WHAT TO DO
- Try to find out what the problem is. If you can't and just have a tearful child who says he hates school, consult his teacher and the school counsellor.
- If the problem is noise or disruption from building, traffic, sports grounds or whatever suggest the teacher uses a lapel microphone and all kids use earphones.

- If bullying is the problem, the school will have policies for addressing the conflict. There are also ways to help kids cope. Read Susanne Gervay's *I am Jack* and go online for more support and information. Bullies invariably have their own major problems, which need to be addressed, for their sake as well as others.

Seeking professional tutoring

One of the most frustrating things for anyone with a dyslexic child is that so many experts have their own pet theory about what causes the disorder and how to overcome it. I have lost count of the number of times I have been told, 'Oh, X is absolutely wonderful! He/she can teach *any* child to read in one/six/twenty easy lessons, by giving them coloured glasses/training their eyes to do such and such/slowing down their focus.'

And, yes, usually these techniques are effective — although often not quite as universally magical as claimed — but *not* for *all* children.

There is no one technique that solves all problems. I wish there was.

Any special education or tutoring *may* help if your child has reading problems, as it teaches children to focus and work out their own problems as they spend more time on the subject. Feeling as though someone cares enough to help doesn't do any harm either.

Sometimes too a learning support teacher speaking slowly and clearly in a quiet room, without distractions, may alone be enough to help children recognise how words are made up of sounds, especially if they come from a family where words are slurred or the TV is always making distracting noises in the background, and how those sounds are put back together to make words. Those two techniques of breaking a word down into its component sounds and then blending sounds to make a word are absolutely crucial — and very difficult for some kids who live in a world of other competing sounds.

Many boys, in particular, process sounds more slowly than girls, and this may be part of the reason that more boys than girls have reading problems. Simply training teachers — or parents — to speak more slowly and distinctly may have a dramatic and positive effect on these boys' ability to learn these skills.

But sometimes tutoring can be harmful, especially if it's done by untrained volunteers. A child who has problems focusing, for example, will need different help from one who is simply a slow learner. One boy I know was given pages of large text, few words and lots of white space in his special-education class for years. This just made him feel even more of a failure, as he couldn't even read a 'baby book'. He had the same form of dyslexia as I do — we find it difficult to focus on single words and have to read quickly to read at all. I find the standard learning support text agonising to read — it's really disorienting for me to try to focus on it. And reading with a finger pointing along the line makes it even worse! (As I mentioned earlier I *can* focus; I just must do it *quickly*.)

Sometimes too children are diagnosed with problems like Attention Deficit Disorder or Attention Deficit Hyperactivity Disorder without thorough investigation. ADD/ADHD does exist, but so do misdiagnoses. I've known children who are much brighter than the other members of their class (and so are bored and daydreaming) and children who are of a 'let's conquer the universe before breakfast' nature — very active children — who have all been lumped together in the ADD/ADHD basket.

This is not the teacher's fault. Teachers almost invariably have far too little time to perform miracles. Even a special-education teacher may not be able to diagnose certain problems, although he or she may be pretty good at working out which experts the child needs to see to get a proper diagnosis.

TUTORS

Many tutors advertise in the phone book and online; some are associated with various methods or companies; and others will work on their own.

Make sure that the tutor is not just a teacher earning extra money, and certainly not just a university or high-school student. Working with children with learning difficulties is not classroom teaching at a slower pace. The person *must have* additional training and experience.

It's important too that the child feels happy with the tutor and really feels that they are making progress. If after two visits your child still doesn't like the tutor, or feels that what they are doing is 'silly', find another tutor. Persisting with one who doesn't suit your child may make her even more discouraged.

ALL TUTORING NEEDS TO BE TAILORED TO THE NEEDS OF THE CHILD. If it doesn't begin to work, or if the child is unhappy about the visit rather than excited about learning, he needs a different tutor and possibly another method of teaching.

JANICE'S STORY

I met Janice five years ago when she was thirteen. I had given a talk at her high school. Her teachers whispered to me before the talk that she was dyslexic and still couldn't read or write. They had been trying to persuade her to learn touch typing and to use a laptop computer, but she was sure it would be no use. She was sure she was dumb and that was all there was to it.

The teachers asked if I'd mind mentioning that I was dyslexic too, even though I'd just had my seventieth book published. So I did, and Janice's teachers coaxed her to talk to me afterwards. I tried to be as inspiring as I could and exaggerated the problems I had at school and have now, and told her that I promised faithfully that if she learnt to touch type and worked at it she'd be reading in three months. (Yes, it was rash, but the girl was desperate.) I said I'd eat my briefcase if she wasn't!

Luckily she didn't take me up on it, because it was four and a half months before I got a letter from Janice, typed on her laptop, with a few spelling errors the spellcheck hadn't been able to understand and so had left uncorrected.

She is doing her first year at university now, studying education. She wants to become a learning support teacher and I think she'll be brilliant at it — as she knows exactly what children with undiagnosed or untreated problems go through.

I still don't know what Janice's problem was. Maybe she doesn't either, although she'll probably find out as she studies the subject. But typing simply made the whole learning process so much simpler, and whatever the problem she was able to overcome it.

CHAPTER 9

TEENAGERS

Teenagers need to learn:
- different ways to use their literacy skills
- how to locate and process information
- more vocabulary, spelling and different styles of writing
- how to find and use the books they love to read or need for study
- how to write different types of long and complex text.

Some teenagers may also need to learn the basic skills they should have been taught earlier (see also How to write an essay on pages 108).

Teenagers who can't read

Tragically, many teenagers can't read even a paragraph. They are the ones passed on by teacher after teacher, up into yet another grade, hoping that someone else will solve the problem. But by the time they are twelve or fourteen they are often classified as 'hopeless'.

They aren't. Everyone can read. But they do need patience and perseverance as by then they will be convinced that they are stupid, and can't read no matter who helps them. They will also be humiliated and possibly have evolved strategies to hide the fact they can't read.

The techniques early in this book work with teenagers, and adults too. But teenagers *must* have material suited to their age, not 'kids' stuff'. They have suffered enough humiliation without being given books about puppy dogs.

Earlier this year I asked teachers to suggest books for teenagers to use as reading aides. All of them offered 'worthy' books: ones that taught moral and social lessons. All were truly good books, but probably not the ones that will make the teenagers so fascinated they are compelled to work at each page to find out what comes next.

Want a book that will lure almost any teenager into reading it? Find a sex manual; not pornography, but one that talks about sex sensibly. No pictures. Blank them out if necessary. Or some of them, so that the teenagers do the reading, and not just browse the illustrations. Choose a book that you feel is suitable to your and their lifestyle, which may not be easy. But 'talking about sex' comes in many, many forms, including material put out by the major religious bodies.

Don't feel comfortable? Which is worse: the kids reading about sex or spending their life deprived of books, the internet, the ability to fill in forms and all the other necessities of modern life? I don't put sex scenes in my books for teenagers — I feel they need a genre that is sex-free. But sex does loom large in their thoughts.

Or OK, let's put sex aside. Look for simple but adult books: you will find a large selection of bestsellers on airport bookshelves, and many bestsellers use very simple language indeed.

Simply giving teenagers guided access to the internet may let them find reading material. But with teenagers, more than any other age, you need to shape their reading matter to fit the student, not your own hopes and expectations, because it is vital — desperate — that they be prompted to work at learning to read, despite all that life has thrown at them that has prevented them from doing so.

Finding time

The most precious resource for most teenagers is time. School pressures and curriculae often leave little time for the kind of reading or creative work that teenagers love best. Many have to put their real interests on hold while they achieve the marks needed to do the subjects they want to study at TAFE or university, or to get the right job. Adolescents and teenagers may also need more sleep because their brains are growing faster than they have since they were toddlers.

Teenagers especially don't have much time to find the books they'd really like to read or to hunt for those books. This is a tragedy. Poring over a wide range of books not only gives teenagers more vocabulary, a better range of expression and many different views on the adult life they have so nearly reached, but they also provide stunningly good downtime in the stress and turmoil of teenage lives. A teenager is learning to be his own person — to survive and find out who he is.

I wish I could give six steps here to help teenagers find more time for the books they love and need. Unfortunately, if those steps exist, I haven't discovered them yet.

Mostly it's a delicate balance between helping — taking books back to the library, being her chauffeur — and turning into a helicopter parent, always hovering.

If you find yourself doing research for your child's projects, for example, *stop at once.* Yes, you are helping your teenager get a higher mark for his assignment right now. But you are also stopping him from learning the skills he'll need as an adult: not just how to research, but how to cope with pressure and deadlines. Coping with pressure and deadlines is an essential skill in the adult world; it is needed to have a successful and fulfilling life.

Give comfort. Give support. Give delicious and nutritious meals, and their favourites before and after exams to show you care and understand. But don't ever do their work for them.

SIGNS YOU ARE HELICOPTERING

- Finding research material for their projects (particularly when they haven't even asked for them).
- Writing to an author for material for a project that has to be in by 9 am the next day and signing it with your child's name (trust me: your writing style probably won't be that of a teenager — we can tell).
- Correcting spelling. Get kids to use the spellcheck. (You're not helicoptering if you are showing them how a spellcheck works.)
- Editing and 'tightening up' an essay, unless you have been asked to do so by its author.

- Encouraging plagiarism, including getting someone else to do the essay to get a good mark; this is not helicoptering, it is actually criminal — and you are teaching your kid that it's OK.

MONITORING PROGRESS

It's not helicoptering to keep an eye on your kid's progress.

- Check up on their essay skills at parent–teacher nights. If they aren't up to scratch, ask the teacher's advice. If necessary, get outside coaching.
- Talk. Adults often claim that their children don't talk to them, but often the adults don't talk to their children either. If your kids aren't talking to you, you may not have talked with them enough. (Talking *to* kids isn't the same as talking *with* them.) Good intellectual and loving relationships between parents and teenagers really do help guide their learning.

How to help teenagers who have missed out

By now, most schools pretty much give up on teenagers who can't read or write fluently, deciding they are 'unteachable' — an excellent way to cop out without anyone having to feel too guilty.

Guilt is good. Guilt makes us look beyond the comfortable and do a bit extra for others. *Everyone* can read. Someone who can't retain a visual image can read Braille. There is no room here to list the hundreds of teenagers I have met who learnt to read fluently, often within a few weeks, after years of failure. Some even taught themselves to read when they were given access to the internet — as I've explained throughout, it's often easier to learn to read by using a keyboard and reading a computer screen. And, for teenagers especially, it is a lot more fun. So ...

GIVE ANY TEENAGER WHO HAS LITERACY PROBLEMS ACCESS TO A COMPUTER

A computer has another major advantage over books, pens and paper: it's embarrassing to go to learning-support lessons, but no one can see you working things out on your own with a computer.

Of course the internet and social media also contain an extraordinarily tempting world. It's often tempting for all the wrong reasons (once again, use guidance here). But being able to access the internet may motivate teenagers when schoolwork and the books available in the school library don't. The world of the internet is *big*, and somewhere in there is the material that will hook the teenager into reading more. And more. And more.

One way of tactfully guiding them is to hunt up sites they may enjoy, from watching a volcano in real time to see if it explodes while they're watching to hunting for the Loch Ness Monster (also in real time). There are fan sites for cricketers, Olympic horse riders and sites that tell you how to build your own computer or chook shed. There are sites aimed at skateboarders and roller-bladers and surfers.

MAKE SURE YOUR KID HAS AN EMAIL ADDRESS!

If you don't have a computer with a modem, take the kid down to the library regularly and book them time on one. This is a fantastic way for teenagers to practise writing and reading, as no one pays much attention to spelling — it's fast, informal, done with your mates and fun.

Encourage kids to email every internet-connected friend and relative you can haul up.

Second-hand computers can be very cheap. But, be warned, they may be filled with junk — malware that's survived a too-perfunctory hard-drive wipe, or worse if it hasn't been wiped at all. Get someone who knows computers to clean up the drives for you before presenting it to your teenager!

ARRANGE FOR PROFESSIONAL TUTORING, HOPEFULLY THROUGH THE SCHOOL

If the school won't help, make a fuss. Ask your friends and relatives to make a fuss too: not for your own child — which will embarrass them — but for all the kids who are missing out if the school doesn't have a good literacy support scheme.

STAND BACK AND LET OTHERS HELP

This is hard. Parents are often the worst possible teachers for a teenager. You fall into the, 'I know best and you will do what I tell you' role all too easily.

A parent's role at this stage is as a support person, not a managing director. You have to be there when they need you and learn to butt out at other times — and perhaps to arrange things so that they get the support they need from other people, whether it be a teacher, tutor or a wider group of friends who share their interests.

BE THERE WHEN THEY DO NEED YOU, AND SO THEY CAN ASK FOR HELP

This probably won't be convenient — they'll want to discuss the meaning of life or how everyone hates them or how quadratic equations are impossible just as you are heading off to bed or trying to take the cat to the vet or ten minutes off staging a major teleconference. But you *do* need to be there, because if you're not there for them at that one critical moment, the moment may pass and never return. We all have public as well as private duties, but unless the fate of the planet or someone's life depends on your being available in the next half hour, make your kids your priority. If you can't be there for your kids, because of distance, illness, lack of mobile reception, encourage them to have a close relationship with someone who can be there, or at least in mobile-phone range.

SET UP TIMES WHEN THEY KNOW THAT THEY WILL NEVER BE PUSHED ASIDE

Lying across the foot of your bed on Sunday mornings, sometimes with the paper, sometimes without; chatting, telling tales and sharing opinions.

GET RID OF EXPECTATIONS

Children never become who you expect: they have their own interests and priorities. This means that the subjects that deeply interest you, from engines to horses, may not be the ones your children love, although they may come to appreciate them later. I worried when my son was young that he was tone deaf because he just didn't like music. He's not tone deaf and he *does* like music, just not the sort that I do, or even the music I loved when I was younger.

It's important sometimes to stop and think when you are helping your children learn, Who am I doing this for, them or me?

Most of us have a good bit of ego wrapped up in our children and we want them to do well so that we feel good about ourselves as well as them. Children who have problems reading need help — no question. Children who are not doing as well as they could, *probably* need help too.

Are they doing as well as they want to? Or is it you who wants them to do better? Are they doing well enough to do the things they want to do when they leave school? If so, do they really need to do more than this? My brother perfected the art of *just* passing every subject he needed, of *just* getting enough marks to get into his BA course, his university honours course, his postgrad diploma, his MA. He said that any more work than necessary was a waste of time. No, he's not an under-achiever — quite the contrary. Instead he was an expert at cost–benefit analysis in his pram (and is now a management consultant and one of the three men whose achievements I admire most).

Children who are bored and unfulfilled will be unhappy; they need coaxing and help to do better. But do make sure that it's their needs you're fulfilling, not your hopes.

(IN A WHISPER) KEEP READING TO THEM

If they're not too embarrassed, especially if they are crook, but don't tell anyone, not even Grandma!

How to help teenagers get books

Hopefully by now your teenager will know where to find books: libraries, bookshops, online bookshops, websites from which they can download books, second-hand bookshops, friends and relatives who don't mind lending (and they'll learn to return them to their owners as well). But they may not have time. It's not helicoptering to be a chauffeur or general delivery service: 'Tell me what you want, i.e., title and author, and I'll hunt it out for you.' This is also a great time to teach teenagers that they can sell their books to raise money for more books.

Have books on hand for them to read and magazines on subjects they enjoy. These magazines may well be aimed at adults — in which case rejoice, as they'll be expanding their vocabulary beautifully. Have this sort of reading around especially in the holidays or at weekends when they have time to browse. You can borrow a new assortment of magazines every couple of weeks from the library, and sooner or later one may grab their attention. Sometimes children don't know what they are interested in because they've never come across it.

Helping teenagers with spelling

This is not the time for the spelling games in earlier chapters. Any help you offer in this department has to be tactful. Incredibly tactful.

- Mention how you adore your spellcheck. The spellcheck is your friend.
- Have Scrabble tournaments during the holidays with genuine prizes — like not doing the dishes for a week for the winner.
- And while the Scrabble set is out, put out a new word every few days that you suspect she is having trouble spelling.
- If you spot a misspelt word on a Christmas card or shopping list and get away with saying, 'Hey, I think it's spelt such and such a way,' without the teenager having a hissy fit — congratulations, you have achieved a good (and rare) learning relationship.

THE STORY OF THE TEENAGERS FROM PELICAN POINT CORRECTIONAL INSTITUTION

Hopefully there's no such place as Pelican Point with any institution whatsoever, because I don't want the kids or the place where they learnt to read identified here. It's enough to say they were teenage boys in a place where kids get dumped when they've broken the law.

There was no funding for literacy programs, even though almost all the kids couldn't read. These were teenagers, right? Everyone knows that if teenagers can't read then they're unteachable.

But, in that strange arbitrary way of funding allocations, there was funding for an art program, because everyone knows that kids who aren't any good at reading enjoy art.

So the kids got computers and internet access for their art lessons. And within three weeks every single boy had learnt to read and was catching up on all the stuff he'd missed; and, yes, much of it wasn't what they needed — or even should have had — because there wasn't the money for anyone to guide them at that stage of their life.

But they did learn to read. Themselves. And if those teenagers can do it — neglected, abandoned, locked away — then anyone can. Especially with a hand to help them.

CHAPTER 10

GETTING KIDS HOOKED ON BOOKS

I met Sam with his dad at a writing workshop I was giving. Sam was enthusiastic all through the workshop, bouncing up and down as we all outlined a story together (it was about a tribe of hippy elephant surfers living on an island in the Great Barrier Reef who were having trouble with the vampire mermaids).

Sam seemed like exactly the sort of kid who devours books at one sitting then demands his parents give him another one … *now*. But his father informed me gloomily afterwards that Sam hated reading.

'Does he have trouble reading?' I asked. Sam had seemed very bright and imaginative for his age, and often it's these kids who do have problems learning to read.

'No,' said Sam's dad. 'He can read very well. He just doesn't like books.'

Sam nodded next to him.

'Maybe he just can't find the sort of books he likes,' I suggested.

Sam's dad got a bit indignant at that. 'His mother and I adore reading. The whole house is filled with books.'

'But are they the sort Sam likes?' I insisted.

'There are all sorts of books there! He can choose whatever he likes! I've still got all the books I loved as a child and so does his mother. We must have every children's classic ever written. *The Lion, the Witch and the Wardrobe, The Wind in the Willows* ...' He was getting quite heated by now.

Sam looked bored.

'Do you have *The Day My Bum Went Psycho?*' I asked.

Sam's head jerked up. A light of fiendish joy appeared in his eyes.

'Sam wouldn't like rubbish like that,' his father declared.

The light went out.

I wish I could give you a happy ending for this one: how I gave Sam's dad a list of ten books and bet him a hundred dollars that Sam would love every one of them and when I won the bet we spent the hundred dollars on the sort of books Sam loved, not the ones his dad thought he *should* love. But it didn't happen like that. Sam's dad stormed off in a huff and Sam trailed after him.

But ... maybe ... there *was* a happy ending. Maybe Sam got a fantastic teacher the next year, or a dedicated teacher librarian who introduced him to books — funny or adventurous books or maybe science-fiction books or thrillers about modern kids in situations Sam could identify with. (Or maybe he just remembered that amazing title and went looking for it himself.)

I have no idea what books Sam would love — even though he was certainly intrigued by a book with 'bum' in the title. He may have been bored after three pages but intrigued enough to look further than his parents' shelves for something else to try — and either way I'd bet far more than a hundred dollars he'd end up loving a lot of books without 'bum' in the title too.

Different kids like different books. And kids who are given the wrong books — even with the very best of intentions — may turn into reluctant readers, even though their reading skills are pretty high level.

Why it's important to give kids the books they love

When I was seven our teacher taught us possibly the most depressing poem in the universe. ... *and I am here, in this world of pain and woe ...*

Umpteen years later it's etched in my mind forever.

Every book a child reads is an important part of his life's experience — and it's a tragedy to waste it on books he hates or is bored or depressed by.

If kids find books are boring, it'll take a lot of good books (or, with luck, one stunningly fantastic book) to change their minds.

How to make kids bored with reading

Usually, when I speak in schools, I ask the teachers to close their eyes and then ask the kids to put up their hands if they don't like reading books. At least 30% of kids put up their hands. And these are in schools where reading is encouraged and books are loved.

Why?

We lose most of our readers from about six onwards, just as they are learning to read. With all the best intentions parents stop reading to their child, and give them simple books to read themselves instead.

Kids need more than the simple books they can read themselves. Kids who are watching complex shows on TV, with clever humour, aren't going to want to read a chapter book instead.

The answer? Keep reading to your kids until they ask you to stop. (They may never ask you to stop. Dad still read bits out to me over the phone when I was in my fifties, and I read out bits to him.)

Read your kids the challenging, exciting books they'll love, but can't quite read: *Lord of the Rings*, or *Harry Potter* ... head to the library and choose at least six books together, then try them all, till you find a book your child is fascinated with.

And cheat, a bit. Leave the book open when you've read a chapter and you may find they read another half chapter themselves, just to see what will happen next, though they'll still want you to read most of it.

But also offer kids books that are written for adults, too. By the time kids are 10–12 they are ready to enjoy the types of books they'll read all their lives, including thrillers and romances.

By seven to ten years old, kids can understand adult shows on TV. We don't say 'you can't watch that' because they don't understand it. We say 'you can't watch that' because we know they will understand it, and it contains themes that are too confronting for them.

Finding good 'adult' books for your kids is harder than giving them books written especially for kids, ones you know won't have sex or violence in them. You'll need to read them first, or at least skim through them.

Or maybe you have favourite books already, that you can lend to your kids. If you enjoy the same TV shows, there's a good chance you might enjoy the same books. Ask friends and relatives for suggestions.

But never condemn kids to the simple books that they are able to read themselves. Keep reading to them! And if you are lucky, one day, when you need it most, they will be there to read to you.

How to help kids find the books they love

ACCEPT THAT KIDS ARE ALMOST ALWAYS DIFFERENT FROM THEIR PARENTS

And the books your kids like will often be different from the ones you love too. This is probably the hardest step for any loving parent — especially one who loves books and reading.

One of our children, for example, read a steady diet of books where one person single-handedly overcomes, etc., etc. They hated books where people *talk* about things, or speculative fiction — exactly the sort of book I love. If I'd tried to stuff them with the books I adore they'd probably hate reading. Listen to your kids and find out what sort of books they love ...

and don't shudder if they want yet another space adventure or book about horses.

BE SNEAKY

Read half stories or chapters! This will tempt kids to read the other half just to see what happens.

DON'T UNDERESTIMATE YOUR KIDS

Often kids are bored because they are only given simple books, or movie tie-ins. (It is very rare to find a really good movie tie-in! There are many good movies made from fabulous books but there are precious few decent books written based on a successful movie.) Too many parents say, 'Oh, little Cedric doesn't like reading,' and give him the next *Star Wars* series or a joke book so he reads *something*. But even if little Cedric finishes it, it won't make him love reading.

Find half a dozen good solid stories at the library for him to choose from, whether they're adventure books or 'chick's books', as my son describes them, with characters and emotions. You need real meat on the hook if you're going to catch a kid!

A funny book can also be a *great* book, like those by Morris Gleitzman, or Terry Pratchett's *The Amazing Maurice and his Educated Rodents*. This is a hilarious book with lots of widdling jokes, but it's also rich and fascinating and will wriggle down into children's minds.

The most sought-after books, such as the *Harry Potter* books, are rich in characters and events and they're *big* too — the sort of book to lose yourself in. If you have absolutely no idea what books your child might like, have a chat with the children's librarian at your nearest large library or the teacher librarian at your child's school.

HELP YOUR KIDS READ WIDELY

I love cherries and chocolate — but I'd hate to have to live on them, even assuming they provided the entire range of nutritional needs. And it is the same with books. It's a real mistake to think that kids will only love one sort of book — that a boy who loves raunchy, rude and fast-paced adventures won't equally love a deeper, more complex book at some other time.

Kids need to be taught that just as you like different foods at different times, so you also like different books for different moods. When he's feeling brain dead after a heavy day at school he may like something light and funny. When he's bored on holidays he might like something deeper that moves him and makes him think.

She may also need to be told that she may not like what her best friend likes, whether it's vampire books or anchovies on her pizza. And even if she doesn't like what most of the rest of the class likes, the world is full of an extraordinary range of books and the ones she will love are out there somewhere.

TEACH KIDS TO BE SUCCESSFUL BOOK HUNTERS

Kids can't read books that aren't there.

It's so easy for kids to turn on the TV but books have to be hunted out — and just like our ancestors had to learn how to hunt a sabre-toothed tiger, it takes time to be a successful book hunter. They already know where to look for books, but do they know how to find the ones they like in shops and libraries? How to assess a book just by skimming the back cover and first page and a bit of the middle? Learning to cut through the shelves full of books they don't like will mean they don't decide there's no such thing as a book they do like. Many of the online book shops have a good 'if you like this then you'll like that' service. They're not infallible, but not bad either.

But if your child does buy a book she hates, don't let her feel she has wasted her money. Someone else will like the book — a friend, or even a charity, so the money will end up in a good cause. Or they may find they like it at another time, when they are older or just feel like that kind of book. Sometimes we feel like pizza, sometimes watermelon — and it's the same with books. Luckily books have a longer shelf life than pizza. Shove it on a shelf, and come back to it.

ACCEPT THAT — LIKE ADULTS — KIDS HAVE THEIR OWN IDEAS ABOUT WHAT THEY ENJOY READING

Many kids don't like fiction. As my grandson said when he was six, he just wanted to read about 'things and stuff'. Many kids go through phases where they just want any escapism (especially if school or other parts of life are stressful) or to immerse themselves in the books of a single author or a subject like dinosaurs or fairies. Go with the flow ... accept they need to read what they want to read, but do make it easy to extend their reading too by providing other books or reading material that they will love! It takes work, persistence and imagination to teach kids that reading is fun.

FIND THE MAGIC BOOK

The 'magic book' is the one that turns non-readers into readers. You know you've found it when your child doesn't want to let it go to sleep or play or eat. When you find the magic book — and it isn't easy — it will so entrance your child that he'll work hard to follow the story even if he can't understand all the words. It will be the book that leads him to another book ... and another ... and another ...

What's its name? I don't know. One member of our family's magic book was *The Lord of the Rings* (long before the movie). Another's was the *Pearlie in the Park* series, which led to two years straight of reading about fairies. One small person's magic book was an (adult's) *Guide to Amphibians of Australia* (for his seventh birthday). Mostly though I know about 'magic books' because parents and teachers write to me that one of my books has been the magic for their kids. I suspect most/many authors get the same kind of letters. There's no one 'magic' book that suits us all.

Look at the winners and shortlisted books of Kids' Choice and Children's Book Council of Australia awards. There may be no 'one' magic book, but some books are much more popular than others. Your child probably won't like every book on the shortlist, but they'll probably *love* one of them.

The book kids grab first may not be the magic book. If you tell your child she *has* to choose a book, she'll probably go for a short funny one. She'll enjoy it, but it's not the magic book unless it leads her to read more and more and more.

Magic books have substance. You get lost in a magic book, and never want to leave. A short funny book is like an ice cream — delicious, but soon gone. The magic book is one that stays with you all your life.

Other people's magic books
See the lists on pages 94–99

- But also: **teach your child to *ask*!** Ask librarians and booksellers — tell them what books they have liked and ask for something similar.
- **Ask other kids** with their/similar interests — horses, football, etc. — if they have read any good books about their passion recently. Ask teachers or the people at bookshops or libraries what are the most popular kids' books around, and then try them!
- Tell them to **ask their best mates.** This is the way most adults find out about good books after all — if our friend says a book is great we tend to read it — but do reassure kids that just because they don't like the same books as their best mate, they may still love books! Also encourage your kids to tell their friends when they find a cool book (or, even better, a series that goes on for several books) so that they can share their enjoyment and sense of discovery with their friends — and, hopefully, create a sense of excitement around the notion of books and reading.
- **Let kids know they can stop reading.** Encourage kids to borrow as many books as possible each time they go to the library — but if they don't like any of them after a chapter and a half, encourage them to *stop reading* and try another ... and another and

another. And take them back to the library pronto
if none of them are worth the effort of ploughing
through.

Forcing a kid to read a book that bores them
is one of the best ways I know to make kids hate
reading. Yes, kids need to be introduced to their
heritage of great literature — but there is a heck of
a lot of great literature in the world, and some of it
will be the stuff your kid will like.

- **Check out comics.** In France some comic books
  are considered classics too. I'd definitely add any of
  the books about Asterix the Gaul and Tintin to the
  classics list!

- **Taste a book!** This is possibly the most valuable
  literacy skill of all. No, you can't judge a book by its
  cover — but covers can still be a help in working out
  if you are likely to like it or not. Leaf through the
  book and look at the style of writing: does the writer
  use a voice — boring, blokey, twee, jokey, romantic,
  etc. — that turns you off?

  Read the blurb on the back. Read a paragraph
  from three separate pages. This will probably be
  enough to let you know if the book has an even
  chance of keeping you turning the pages.

  Most adults have already learnt this technique —
  but it's a great help if someone else teaches it to you
  early!

- Teach kids to keep a **list of books** they like so they
  can hunt out more by that author. I tend to discover
  an author then go through a lovely time reading
  absolutely everything they've written. All libraries
  and bookstores can look up on their computer
  systems to tell you what other books an author has
  written and if they are available. *All* libraries can
  order books in from other libraries — it's called an
  inter-library loan — and *all* bookshops can order
  a book in for you if the publisher is still selling it.
  If not, contact a good second-hand bookstore and
  they'll hunt round and find it for you — usually for
  less money than it would cost new, unless it is a very
  old or rare edition.

- Ask if you can put up a **suggestion box** at your
  local library, so that all library members can ask for
  books they'd love to see on the shelves — then teach
  your kid to look at book review pages, bestseller
  lists, kids' magazines, kids' websites and the
  websites of their favourite authors to find out what
  new books are coming out that they may love —
  then bung a suggestion into the box fast!

- Introduce your **favourite books** to your child.
  Sadly this hardly ever works — but it might. Back
  off fast, and don't be disappointed if it's a flop. At
  least you've shown your child that you loved books
  when you were her age. But there are now so many

glorious kids' books, and many older ones have dated badly.

- Suggest your kids start a **book-swap club** at school — one day a month kids bring in books they'd like to swap. Every kid can bring one book in and take one book out — but the book has to be in good condition! Someone (perhaps the school) will need to add a 'starter' to the books though — a few extra books in case a few kids simply can't find anything they like!

Why a good book will always be more vivid than TV

TV is passive — you just sit there and watch. But with a book *you* imagine the place the gorgeous hero or heroine is being held to ransom — and your imagination will always come up with something better than the TV version. And, because you are part of creating it, a book will *always* be more vivid.

Test this: ask your kids to read a book and watch a TV show — then ask them three weeks later which they remember best. (But they have to love both the TV show *and* the book or it doesn't count!)

Books give you *words*. Many hilarious books just aren't funny when adapted for TV, because they depend on the side-splitting way the words are put together. Funny words, beautiful words, images that strike right through your heart — more than anything else, humans are creatures that *talk*, and we do love our words and the way they are put together — and while TV will give you funny words too, they won't be as powerful or as plentiful as in a book.

Non-fiction magic

For many kids — maybe about one in five — the magic book will be non-fiction.

My favourite story about a child like this is a friend of my son's — let's call him Paul.

At the age of twelve, according to his teacher and the reading coach his parents had hired, Paul was unable to read more than a few words and his writing wasn't much better. He would stare out the window, he wouldn't concentrate on the subject at hand and reading just seemed beyond him.

Paul was a farming child. His parents had a large mixed farm, but Paul's real passion was chooks. He and my son were trying to cross Australorps with Araucanas to produce a chook that regularly laid large blue eggs.

One day when Paul was at our place I received a veterinary textbook on chook diseases in the mail; we are talking a large book here, tiny text, a real textbook, though it did have good photos. So I gave it to Paul, thinking he'd like to leaf through it.

He clasped it to his chest, sat down with it and four hours later was still reading it. He muttered, 'I haven't quite finished it yet,' when his mum came to pick him up, so I let him borrow it. He left with it still clasped to his chest. Three days later he rang me to say he'd finished it but could he read it again? Actually, I don't think I ever did get it back.

Paul just didn't like fiction — especially the type of fiction so often given to problem readers. And no one had thought to give him stuff he *was* interested in. Paul discovered farming magazines such as *Australian Poultry* magazine and a hoard of books on the topic he was interested in. And he kept on reading, although not, I have to say, in school. (He left at the earliest legal date, but is doing extremely well anyway.)

WHAT TO DO

- Offer your child non-fiction books that provide information about 'real' people and things, not 'pretend' ones. There are great books for children, e.g., Anthony Hill's *Soldier Boy*, that are true stories and will make a non-fiction-loving child understand that they are reading about the real world, not fantastical books with horses and people discussing their feelings.
- Give your child magazines about her favourite subject, or a range of magazines on different topics so that she can find out which subjects she's

interested in. It doesn't matter if these are magazines aimed at an adult audience — if she's interested, she'll work it out. Or try reading half of an article to her so that she knows what it's about, then let her read the rest. She'll now know what the difficult words are likely to be, from *V8-engine* and *foul-brood disease of bees* to *estuarine species of fish*.

Head to the non-fiction section of the library. Try the kids' section first, but then the adults, as the 'magic book' may well be there: a motorcycle manual, a book on beekeeping, reference books on slithery things or those with scales.

- Find websites about interesting subjects and show them how to browse. Then let them find stuff they like. (You will need to include a bit of guidance or maybe censorship here.) Undirected browsing is a surprisingly good way for children to pick up reading skills — as long as there is an adult keeping an eye out for exactly what they reach.
- Give your child a newspaper every day and read a few items with him — if your child isn't interested in current affairs he might instead enjoy articles in the motoring, sports or fashion sections.
- Encourage kids to read out bits from newspapers or magazines to you (maybe when you are preparing the evening meal). You'll find out what they're

interested in. Your kids will also feel they're helping to educate you and you'll find fertile ground for discussion. It's a lovely, companionable way to spend twenty minutes together.

- Give children recipe books — the ones with great colour pictures of each dish — and let them work out what they want for dinner. You'll be amazed how many children will ponder all the hard-to-read ingredients to make sure that they don't include coconut or pumpkin or whatever they particularly hate. The reward, of course, is that they get to choose what's for dinner the next day.

- Don't be afraid to give kids books or magazines aimed at an adult audience. Many children who prefer non-fiction don't like 'kids' stuff'. Histories and biographies are a fabulous source of reading material, and once kids are reading eagerly and fluently, it's amazing how they can be tempted by some other types of fiction as well.

Don't worry if a child chooses something that you consider to be too complicated or sophisticated. Most children practise a form of censorship of their own, glossing over the bits that make no sense to them yet and concentrating on the bits that do make sense. And don't worry too much about unsuitable adult material either — people process words differently from pictures, especially moving images. Censor what your child is allowed to watch on film or television, but let him read whatever he wants to, as long as it wouldn't be R- or X-rated if it were a DVD.

A child allowed to read *All Quiet on the Western Front* won't be spooked by gruesome images in the same way that one who watches a violent film might be. She will be haunted by big questions about violence and war and the randomness of history and how people's lives are changed by other people's decisions, but these are quite appropriate questions to be haunted by. *However*:

- do be there to answer questions or give comfort
- do read a bit of whatever your kid is reading, in case he is affected by what he reads
- if the book does have an unhappy or emotionally demanding ending, make it a 'morning only' book, not to be read before bedtime (in case of nightmares)

KIDS NEED CHALLENGING BOOKS, WITH CHALLENGING THEMES, BUT ALWAYS WITH AN ADULT TO GUIDE THEM THROUGH.

And as for 'big words', as long as they can understand eight words in ten, they'll pick it up — especially if they feel comfortable asking you to tell them what the really hard words are.

CHAPTER 11

FAMILY READING

For many kids reading is something you do at school or for homework — i.e. because it's supposed to be good for you, like Brussels sprouts. For others it's something to do when there's nothing on TV, and their brother's hogging the computer.

Kids need to learn that reading can be a social activity as well as a solitary one — and something that's fun to do together instead of just good for them!

Years ago, in the world before DVDs, there were public readings — people with well-trained voices and a dramatic manner who'd read stories to a whole hall of people. I suppose the book readings on ABC Radio are the same thing in different clothes.

It's possible, without being so weird that they make TV documentaries about you ('... and after the news, a family that *reads*!'), for the whole family to enjoy books together, just like they sit round the TV together. (I bet that in ten years' time you won't remember a single evening spent around the TV, but you'll remember the reading together with love and happiness — and possibly a few retrospective giggles too.)

Given that you'll get so much pleasure from family reading, it seems a bit mean to add that there will be literacy advantages too — not just the reading practice kids get, but the feeling that reading is something to enjoy, not work at, and that it's something that people they love and admire — i.e. you — enjoy as well. Plus there's an ego boost in knowing you are both enjoying the same sort of book, instead of them reading kids' stuff and you reading something for grown-ups.

Family reading is especially valuable to the child who is having problems with reading, too, as it *is* fun stuff. But for less confident readers you can try:

- choosing a favourite book you have read to them at least once before, so they know what the difficult words (like earthquake or wizard) are in advance
- reading alternate pages or even paragraphs with them — again, this will give them most of the words they may find in the next page or paragraph and make the challenge much easier
- reading long sections of speech or interviews with sports people or musicians that they like; many kids

get a bit of a buzz pretending to be their hero or heroine, and reading their words for them

- writing down a story they tell you one night, then getting them to read it to you the next night — or you reading it to them the second night and they reading it to you the third night

(This is even more of an ego boost, as you can tell them it's such a stunning story you can't wait to hear it again and, as by now they will know it almost by heart, it will make reading it aloud far easier.)

P.S. If kids don't like reading aloud, *don't* ask them to. You read aloud to them while they do their chores and wait till they say, 'How about I read while you stack the dishwasher?'

What and when to read together
PLAYS AND OTHER PLEASURES

When I was a kid my mother and I used to read plays together — she'd take some parts and I'd take others and it was a lot of fun.

It was also very easy reading! Mostly I'd only have to read a line or so at a time and because Mum was reading the same book too she mostly read out the difficult words before I had to work out what they were.

Not all kids like reading plays aloud — some will find it almost as embarrassing as kissing their mums goodbye in public. But some kids can find it a real joy.

By the time I was ten I was writing plays for my younger brothers and sister. Their favourite was *The Headless Hound*, a puppet show about a headless dog — well, he had to be headless as the baby had pulled his head off and chewed it.

As well as giving kids reading practice, reading plays aloud encourages kids to put on performances for you and any other adult who can be tempted to take a seat. It'll give them confidence to talk in public, and help them learn to speak clearly and with expression.

But most of all, it will be something they can do themselves — or with you, their brother and sister or their friends — and feel proud of, instead of sitting like a blob in front of the TV absorbing someone else's pretend life.

READING TO ENTERTAIN THE WORKERS

Take it in turns to read or do the washing up, or read aloud and tidy the room — one person works, the other person reads to entertain them and then you change places.

Choose books that everyone will love for this. Funny books or short stories or crazy poems like

Revolting Rhymes, Roald Dahl's hilarious retelling of fairy tales. *The Lord of the Rings* is a great standby — you'll get years of housework done while that is being read out!

P.S. Even a reluctant reader may be less reluctant to read aloud if it means someone else does the tidying!

FAMILY POEMS

Kids mostly love poetry — the rhythm of it and the song in the words. Kids as young as four have fun finding rhymes for words and putting rhymes together.

Make it a family habit to write a poem for everyone on his or her birthday or to write a special Christmas poem about what the year has been like. They don't have to be long complex poems — a limerick is fine:

> *There once was a kid called Brett*
> *Who rode on his bike for a bet ...*

Or if their name is Samantha or Bartholomew or something else that's hard to find a rhyme for:

> *It's Samantha's birthday today*
> *And so I would just like to say ...*

And of course they can be a lot ruder, and if kids are doing them they probably will be; they can even put them to music to embarrass their brothers or sisters in forty years' time.

But basically it's fun and it's making them feel at ease playing with words and giving them confidence that words are theirs to use — and this confidence will stand them in good stead when the poems and songs are cherished memories.

P.S. I was at an eightieth birthday party last year, and the kids — now middle-aged — all read out some of the ruder birthday poems they'd written for their brothers and sisters forty-odd years ago. It was happy and hilarious and by the end of the afternoon their own grandkids were scribbling down poems to be read in another half-century's time!

LOO POEMS

As mentioned earlier, a friend's loo is papered with family poems, limericks and jokes, plus the odd reminder to *You know who: Don't forget to wash your hands. No — wet hands aren't the same as clean hands. You have been WARNED! Love, Mum.*

There's a family rule that you can only paste over someone's poem after it's been there for six months, then it's fair go. Luckily there's a surprising amount of wall space in a loo, especially now Tim can reach the ceiling on a stepladder. It really is the most interesting loo I know.

P.S. If it's a rented house, hang butcher's paper from the ceiling and Blu-Tack poems etc. to that.

OTHER POEMS

Poetry — the sort that rhymes, has rhythm and preferably tells a story — is often easy reading for kids. The short lines and the rhymes help you predict what the next word will be.

Look for simple poems to begin with, like Roald Dahl's *Revolting Rhymes*. Once kids are reading fluently though you may find they love other poems — as a very young child I loved poems like 'The Lady of Shalott' or 'The Forsaken Merman' or 'The Man from Snowy River' — poems that told stories. Or ones like 'Break, Break, Break' that I loved just for the sound of the words and the bright images they gave me.

Poems are also *fast* — you can read most out in the time it takes to stack a dishwasher and you get a heck of a lot of beauty or profundity per second — a most cost-effective use of time for active kids.

Like all reading matter, you'll need to match the poem to the child — and encourage them to taste different kinds of poems too. But for most humans a good poem is a rich experience — a bit like a piece of passionfruit sponge cake with cream and fresh strawberries with Great Grandma — you don't want too much, but it becomes a delight and a memory to keep with you for years.

CAR BOOKS

I get carsick if I read in a car, and so do most/many kids. But car trips are great times to put on tapes/ listen to CDs of spoken books — you can borrow them free from the local library. Or make your own tapes/recordings on an MP3 player — everyone in the family can take turns reading part of a story — it's fun waiting to hear your turn. And even more fun if you organise it so that no one has read the entire story — just the bits they read into the tape deck/ microphone!

READING WHEN YOU'RE SICK

Most sick people need cosseting — a feeling they are being loved and looked after. I don't know anything as cherishing as being read to, no matter what your age and even if the book is *Green Eggs and Ham* and you are forty-five and the reader is six and needs help with the big words.

Encourage kids to read to anyone who's feeling crook (assuming it's not desperately infectious or the invalid needs sleep more than entertainment). Kids need training in how to show compassion too!

DIARIES

A few rare kids keep diaries most of their lives. Most keep diaries on and off — and get great pleasure reading them years later.

Diaries, of course, give kids reading and writing practice, as well as preserving not just memories, but also a record of, 'Good grief, did I ever really feel like that?'

Encourage kids to keep diaries but don't pressure them — kids have too many pressures as it is. But a small decorative book is a great way to tempt kids to keep a diary just for their holidays or over Christmas or for the first weeks at a new school or of the school year. Explain that they'll find the diary a fascinating record of their own history when they are older. (Do not say, 'But this diary will help your writing and reading so much. Not to mention your essay construction too. Now how much have you written in your diary today? Can I read it? No, that's not how you spell interfering fossilised old dinosaur ...')

The books kids shouldn't have

There are some books that kids shouldn't have.

I'm not saying some books shouldn't be published. I am saying that parents, teachers and librarians should make sure that *some* kids shouldn't get *some* books.

DEPRESSING BOOKS

Kids should not be given depressing books. A depressing book is one that makes the reader think there is no hope. This is different from a sad book. Many kids enjoy a bit of a cry — especially happy kids.

Many kids' books that are ostensibly marketed for kids are really targeted at the adults who will buy them. They may be brilliant books, but are too dark and depressing for kids. They are really just books for adults that have kids as the main character.

It's easy to move an audience by portraying depressing things — Oh dear, the reader will think, I feel so terrible after reading this book. It has had such a profound influence on me it must be a great book!

It isn't. It is *easy* to move the reader by being depressing. It is much harder to move a reader to tears of joy — though it can be done.

It is also very tempting to think that a depressing book is somehow more 'real' than a joyous one. It isn't. Sad things and joyous things are both only part of life's experiences — and a book which is totally one or the other is *not* realistic. And any book that teaches kids that there is no way out is criminal. Kids need to learn that no matter what bad things happen, there is always hope.

BOOKS THAT LIE

Books can lie about many things. I dislike books that lie about history.

Did you ever see the movie *The Dish*? It's about how the world received the first images of the moon landing from Parkes in Australia — except it's a lie. It didn't happen. And now most people who have seen it think it was true. (It actually happened at Honeysuckle Creek, but the 'dish' had been dismantled there so the filmmakers set it in Parkes instead, where there was a good big dish to film.)

A good historical novel doesn't *change* history. It works around it — writes in between the lines, so someone reading it knows more about what really happened at the end. Books that change history and leave kids thinking the false information is true should be … ahem. I mustn't get carried away there.

Books can lie about all sorts of things — about how people act, about the way the world is. And any lie to a kid is wrong. (I'd class *The X-Files* as a lie — or it is to many kids anyway, because so many actually believe that there is a conspiracy to hide the aliens who've invaded earth. Go ask a few classes to put their hands up if they think there are aliens on earth and the government is lying about them, and see how many stick up their hands. Frightening …)

Fantasy, on the other hand, isn't a lie, because kids don't believe it. Fantasy is suspended disbelief. I don't know any ten-year-old who believes in fairies — though lots wish they did exist! But a heck of a lot believe in aliens. And government conspiracies. (And, no, to any kid reading this, I am not a government agent paid to make people think there are no aliens and no cover-ups. I promise! May the little green men who landed on my rose garden last night chew my toenails if I tell a lie.)

REALISTIC BOOKS (SOMETIMES)

Kids need to learn about the world — and fiction is a great way to do it. But sometimes realism can be too confronting for particular kids at certain stages of their lives.

(Which is why I set my most confronting books in the past, close enough to make kids think and maybe look at their own age with new eyes — but far enough away not to be too grimly real.)

Books with grim realism can be a great experience for kids. But they can also be frightening or depressing, if given at the wrong time. Use your judgement.

The last thing a kid who has been abused or suffered great loss needs is a book to 'identify with'. These kids need escape — not more of the same in book form! Often it's the happiest, most secure kids who can best cope with gritty realism.

On the other hand of the greatest tests of maturity is being able to empathise with others — to break out of the eggshell of just being 'me' and think about others, put yourself in their place ... and reading reasonably realistic fiction is a great way to help learn this. *Some* kids need more realism than others.

SHALLOW BOOKS

These are 'OK' books, the sort that follow a genre someone else has made popular. At the moment they are vampire and zombie books, and books with *fart* prominently in the text, but by the time this book comes out a new fad will probably have got going.

The idea behind these books is that *The Farting Vampire Pirates of Grumblebum Island* has been a success. Therefore, kids love books about farting pirates. Therefore give them more of them — they're often produced cheaply and look it.

There is a reason great and classic books sell lots of copies over many years — people *like reading them*!

Always go for quality with a kids' book: go for awards and kids' choice shortlistings and books that came out five or ten years ago and are still in print. They've lasted, so they must have kid appeal. (Not to every kid, of course. Sigh. You'll still have to do the 'Now what does *this* kid like?' assessments. Life would be much easier if kids were born with their literary genetic codes tattooed along their legs: *This kid will like the following authors. Check the manual to decode. Conditions apply. Battery not included. Serving suggestion only.*)

Giving a kid a 'shallow' book cheats them of the much more profound influence a really *good* book can have. But a funny book — and one aimed at the things kids find funny — can also be a brilliant book. Have a look at Tim Winton's *The Bugalugs Bum Thief*. Andy Griffiths' and Terry Denton's *Treehouse* series is super light, but also brilliant and funny.

BORING BOOKS

An adult can read — or not read — a boring book and forget about it. Each book though is proportionately so much more of a child's experience — and every book they hate teaches them that books are boring!

The saddest letters I ever get are from kids who write: *Our teacher said we had to write to our favourite author and it had to be you because we've studied your book all term and the rest of the class liked it but I fell asleep love Jason. P.S. Couldn't you write a book with a kid called Jason in it and all these laser cannons and a space war?*

I know it's tough work having kids reading different books in a class — but books are something that kids should love, and forcing them to read books when they don't like them isn't going to change their minds. (On the other hand coaxing them to read the first chapter of a book that's different from the ones they usually like is quite a different thing!)

Have a shortlist of books for kids to choose from or get kids to vote on a proposed book for study and drop the ones that any kid is likely to really hate! Or give them special dispensation to study their own books — warn them it'll take a lot more work on their parts (they won't care if it means more work for the teacher, though maybe that could be tactfully mentioned just to speed up their social-consciousness-raising).

TERRIFYING BOOKS

Kids are scared of different things from adults. Bullies, the dark, fear of being abandoned — all are much more terrifying to a child than an adult.

It may seem that no child should ever be given a terrifying book. But sometimes giving a child a book shows them how to conquer the things they are scared of — and as the child identifies with the hero or heroine, they'll actually be doing the conquering in their imagination. Some of the most successful (by any and all criteria) kids' books are ones where kids overcome bullies, burglars, intergalactic villains, evil wizards. Just make sure the good guys win, and no kitten gets hurt or faithful dogs wounded for readers below say ten years, and it will all just be a pleasant tickle of the terror buds.

In other words terror is fine, as long as it's 'happy terror' and doesn't verge into 'I can't cope with life' terror, where it is all too hard, too frightening — that's depression.

SEX

Kids are usually bored or grossed out by sex scenes until they are old enough to want to read material with overt sex scenes. Usually they'll skip over sex scenes (which I did with all the adult books I read as a young child — I was quite surprised when I read them later as an adult to find there was any sex in them) or go read another book if there's too much to skip over.

I avoid writing about sex in my books for kids and young adults. Young adults read as many books written for adults as they do ones written for their own age group, and have access to any number of sex scenes in books in libraries or on TV. In this era when everything from soft drink to jeans are sold by using sexual images, it's good for kids to have a refuge from an over-sexualised world. But if and when they do want those sex scenes in their books, parental guidance is recommended. Explain that when you are young anything you read or watch can influence the way you feel about the world, and this includes sex. Is it depressing? Cruel? Violent? Frightening? Is anyone hurt by what happens? Then avoid it.

VIOLENCE

If we're talking about villains being covered by lava from a volcanic explosion, no worries. But if we are talking about the kind that might teach kids that violence is an acceptable — or even the best — way to get out of a situation then it's not good food for anyone.

Even worse is where the hero kills three hundred bystanders just to get the villain — which happens in just about every goodies and baddies movie I have seen in the past decade. This teaches kids — and adults too — that it doesn't matter who gets in the way as long as you achieve your goal. And that is terrifying.

A quick guide to what to read when

On a plane trip or at times of extreme possible boredom: think gripping fiction, preferably long so you can stay in that world till the journey is over.

The dentist when you know there'll be drilling; hospital or before the first day at a new school: the next in a familiar and much-loved series or by a favourite author: a total treat book.

On holiday: thick but light to begin with; thick but with layers of meaning as your brain restores itself.

When unhappy: comfort books, where everyone is secure or becomes so. If necessary, check the back of the book to make sure there is a happy ending.

After school: light, escapist, possibly funny.

Before bed: a familiar, light and happy book so you won't want 'just another chapter' and lose sleep.

A PASSPORT TO READING

Every night: read a story at bedtime.

Every dinner time: ask your kids what they're reading, and why they like it, or suggest ways they might find a book they like more.

Once a week: share a household chore like unpacking the dishwasher or tidying their bedroom — one person works while someone reads to them.

Once a week: visit the library together and hunt for books you might like to read. (You don't have to read them all!)

Every weekend: share what you're reading with your kids. Share an item in a newspaper or magazine, or a text from a friend, or an online article.

Every weekend: find a new way to share a book or a poem or a story. Get Grandma to read a story via Skype. Blu-tack up a poem in the loo. Read the dog a bedtime story. Tell the kids a funny story about your childhood, or their grandparents.

Every week: lend a family friend a book you love.

CHAPTER 12

BOOK GROUPS FOR EVERYONE

Adults like reading groups — meeting to talk about a book, eat sticky buns and gossip. Kids love them even more. A book group is a party, but a party with a purpose — the sort of party you remember long after any memory of jumping castles has faded.

Book groups for littlies (3 months to school age)

It doesn't matter how young kids are — they will still enjoy a book group.

How to do it: Parents meet once a week or fortnight with their kids. Each parent brings a book to read and a plate of something to eat and each adult takes it in turn to read a book to the assorted kids while the other adults gossip and stop little Mikey from eating Jessica's stuffed rabbit.

The group can meet either at each house in turn or at a library or anywhere that will donate space and maybe a tea urn. (Libraries are great as you can borrow the books there for the day.)

Result: kids get exposure to lots of books; they learn that stories are fun even if they're not sitting on Mum's or Dad's lap; and they learn that other kids like books too. And if it's at the library they learn that book-filled places are fun places to be.

And, of course, in between the books the kids get to play and eat stuff and the adults get a break from being at home with only preschoolers for company.

P.S. Little kids love to participate when you read to them. If the book has a rabbit in it, make them rabbit ears or give them pink rabbit noses and whiskers with face-painting pens and have them hop around in a circle before and after the book. If the book talks about a big elephant and a small ant, show them how to make big and little gestures.

Try a theme day — read books about animals and the children come as their favourite animal, or machines and they bring a toy one. But if you don't have the time, energy or stamina for any of this —

and few parents with under-fives do — just bring the book, eat the bun — and read ...

Reading groups for early readers

This is great for weekend afternoons or school holidays. It works with between two and ten parents.

Each week (or fortnight or day for that matter — if it's a long boring holiday — cold or wet) choose who will bring the book. It's best if it's one none of the kids has read. Again, bring a few buns, plates of fruit, drinks, etc., to make it a party as well.

The adults take it in turns to read a chapter of the book. It doesn't matter if the book isn't finished that session — it can be finished at home, either by the parents or, even better, by the kid, who can't wait to see what will happen next. Again, it's easier for a kid to read a book when they know what it's about and what the more unusual words in it are going to be.

P.S. Series books are excellent for this — if the kid falls in love with one of them, she'll really work at reading the next and the next and the next. And be genuinely disappointed when they run out!

Primary school reading groups

These are school book groups. They can be a group of kids who meet at lunchtime just because they love books and stories, or with an energetic teacher or librarian. There can be several book groups, according to who is interested in what:

- The Adventure Reading Group
- The Horse Book Readers
- The Sci-Fi Readers (the New Worlders?)
- The Comic Club (i.e. comic format, not necessarily hilarious books)
- The Giggle-a-Minute Book Club (devoted to books that have you rolling on the floor by the end of page one).

The book can either be chosen by one of the group or the group can vote on a book or the teacher or librarian can choose one they think the kids would like — which is usually the best bet, as they'll know what books are around.

Option 1: the kids read the book and discuss it at the meeting.

Option 2: the adult can read the book to the kids or the kids can take turns reading it out and then maybe have a short discussion or just give the book a mark out of ten and give reasons for the mark.

Option 3: the group can swap books or comics for the next week — this is probably the best strategy for the comic group, who'll love getting their grubby mitts on more comics but also want to spend most of their lunch hour galloping in sixty directions at once.

P.S. If possible have free popcorn (done in the microwave — it's pretty cheap and fairly healthy too) or sliced watermelon (who cares about the drips) or cups of fruit punch to make it clear that this is fun, not schoolwork!

Teenage book club

Like primary school book groups, this can be a group of particular friends who decide to have a 'book group' once a week or once a month, or ones designed by adults to tempt the teenagers into reading more widely — or just relaxing from the tensions of teenagehood with fiction. The most successful teenager book club I knew met at a café, and the dedicated teacher paid for the coffee. Both the venue and the coffee made it feel like an adult not a school activity. You may even find a cafe that is deslighted to become a book club/coffee club on Tuesday mornings.

If the teenage book club is in the school library, try to give it a non-school feel: coffee (you need not tell them if it is decaffeinated) platters of cheese and fruit or if possible, pizza.

Warning: teenagers can clam up in the presence of the opposite sex. It is better to say nothing than say something embarrassing. While I'd never advocate having single-sex book clubs, having several going at the same time with different genres — a sci-fi book club, or another where each chooses the next book to discuss — may mean that they become predominantly male or female, with the few 'others' leavening things up rather than making everyone self-conscious.

When they meet they can:

- talk about books they love and nominate a book to read the following week to talk about (make sure though the library has multiple copies in that case)
- swap or lend books — in which case accept that teenagers often don't like reading what you want them to read. But before you get too shocked remember what they've seen on TV and at the movies lately
- raise funds so each participant can buy a book — one *they* want. Put their names in their books and keep a register of who owns what book and who has borrowed it.

The books are now swapped round each week.

This type of book group only works with close friends who trust each other with their books. A book can be a much-loved possession and there needs to be a contingency plan to replace lost books, if the teenager who loses it isn't able to pay for it.

CHAPTER 13

A CLASSROOM REVOLUTION

Imagine a classroom — kids sitting quietly at their desks, writing or listening to their teacher talk, or reading what's on the blackboard. This is the way we were educated and the way we expect our kids to be educated too.

But is it the best way?

The way kids are taught today is a relic of medieval schools, where sitting still was regarded as good for the character, teaching the student to submit to authority. Students in ancient Athens, on the other hand, learnt while walking, or with pointers in pits of sand. Kids hate being shut indoors all day. They hate having to sit for hours on end — plus it is bad for a human's health to sit still for so long.

How we fail our kids

One in four Australian children don't make the international literacy benchmark for their age. In the Northern Territory, more than forty per cent of kids between nine and fourteen years don't meet the minimum literacy levels for their age group. Much of this is because of high truancy rates — kids don't go to school. How many other kids wouldn't go to school either, if they had a choice?

We are failing our children. Why? Yes, schools can always do with more money, but by international standards we put a reasonable amount towards education. Our top ten per cent do very well indeed: Australia outperforms in international literary awards, bestsellers innovation and Nobel prizes per head of population.

What can we do better? How?

Kids are natural learners. That is what being a kid is: a small sponge who wants to soak up how the world works. It's why kids ask you a thousand questions when you're in the middle of ironing something made of silk or trying to remember where you parked the car.

In the last three months as part of my national laureate project for 2014–2015, I have been asking kids what they'd like to see changed about school. Try asking your kids what they'd change. The answers may surprise you. Even kids who you think like their schools may talk about how they hate being confined inside all day without moving about, not being able to talk in class, not having enough time to work on their own projects, having to read books that bore them.

Here are some of the suggestions. Some — like a rainbow to take you to school — aren't practical, or not until the daydreaming kid becomes an engineer and works out the details. Others, like lessons in the swimming pool, seem crazy — until you think, just sometimes, this might work. Others make so much sense you can't believe that they haven't been thought of before.

Sam (NT): *School should start at 4 pm. My brothers stay up late so I have to too and don't wake up till ten and then I get into trouble so I don't go to school. By 4 o'clock all the fun stuff has been done and if the school gave us afternoon tea it'd be good to sit there and learn for a while.*

Comment: in rural communities like Sam's, could school begin at 4 pm? Do we have to have a single time to start and end school? Many countries overseas have staggered lesson times. It works.

Sam (ACT) wants more time to work on his inventions. He is five and three-quarters and is inventing a machine to mine asteroids.

Comment: Invention is one of the keystones of our economy and being human. And yet there is no place at school for kids to invent things. They can make things, but not create and invent them.

Emma (Qld) wants a dress-up library so that when you go to school you can choose a tiara or fairy wings to wear all day.
Comment: Why not? Emma bounced with joy at the idea of choosing a 'dress-up' every day.

Emily (Qld) wants teenagers to design their next year's school uniform each year.

Harry (Vic) wants excursions by rocket to other planets but will settle for a school telescope.
Comment: Again, why not? The telescope bit anyway.

Riley (Vic) wants a remote control in your ear for all school devices. He also wants time and resources at school to invent one.

Tahlia (Vic) wants temporary tattoos every time you have been kind and helpful.

Millie and Fleur (Vic) want trampoline school floors.

Josephine (Vic) wants to have classes to make small cars that will run on the school oval.

Jaden (Vic) wants a school shop where you can sell things you grow or make, and buy things too.

Darby (Vic) wants classrooms shaped like dinosaurs.
Comment: Why not get the kids to transform them into dinosaurs or their choice of animal?

Sam (Vic) wants to teleport to school or for daily excursions.

Noah (Vic) wants schools where 'people live and do things not just learn'.

Eric (Vic) wants no homework. He also wants school pets.

Samantha (Vic) also wants pets at school.
Comment: Kids — and adults — are often happier, more focused and relaxed with animals and greenery. I've known schools with school chooks, a school dog, and one that acts as a 'puppy walker' for guide dogs in training. Looking after animals is a superb way to teach kids compassion and nurturing.

Ava (Vic) wants school to be a farm where you pick things to eat.
Comment: I agree.

Lachlan (Vic) wants a dance studio at school to teach dancing at breaks.
Comment: The one school I know that has this has the best focused and 'debounced' kids I have ever seen.

Chelsea (Vic) wants a free lunch canteen.
Comment: Other countries have free lunch programs for kids who need them. I have known too many kids in Australia who would be hungry if other kids didn't share their lunch with them. This may be more neglect than poverty, but whatever the cause, school food is a cure. A

school breakfast and after-school care snack — a nutritious one — can also make an enormous difference to kids.

Darren (Vic) wants lessons in a swimming pool.

Ryan (Vic) wants an electro board instead of a desk.

Jordan (Vic) wants a skateboard park.

Amelia (Vic) wants charms for a bracelet every year when you do something really good, so you can have a new bracelet every year.

Amelia (Tas) wants more chooks.

Kelly, year 9 (Qld) wants a crèche for teachers' babies, where you can learn to look after kids.

Jayden and three others (SA) want more ropes and cricket bats in the sports library.
Comment: Their school already has a library of sports equipment kids can borrow before and after school and at lunchtime, but the kids wanted more.

Duane (Qld) wants things to make forts with.

Lexie (WA) wants to be able to explain problems in class to her best friend.

Cara (Vic) wants safety lessons on a roller coaster.

Lexis (ACT) wants a test for teachers every year that asks: Do you like kids and teaching? If they say 'no' they are given another job.

No kid is hopeless

I have lost count of the number of times I have been told 'They're hopeless', 'There's nothing you can do with kids like these', 'There's no point turning up, really'. Two years ago I had to bet a headmistress $5,000 that I could 'keep the kids under control' before she'd let me speak to the assembled school. She didn't take the bet, and the teenagers were almost motionless for the entire hour's talk. It was possibly the first time anyone had spoken to them as human beings, telling them that they had a choice: or accept the expectations of their teachers and even parents, or to face the challenges of life head on. I couldn't promise them a perfect world, or even that they'd fulfil their ambitions. But I could promise that if they got stuck into it, they'd never, ever be bored again.

If a teacher says any of the phrases above, more than once a week (everyone is allowed to let off steam — especially teachers) it is time they left face-to-face teaching, and took another job in education. A teacher like that has the potential to cause far more harm than good. Yes, we need more, and different, teacher training, especially in literacy. We also need a system that rewards passionate teaching. I have never known a passionate teacher fail with any child.

And most teachers *are* passionate, doing far more than the basics their job requires. Nearly all can be brilliant teachers in a system that supports and rewards inspired teaching. This doesn't have to be with money: I know of one school in a poor area where most parents are recent immigrants to Australia, and where learning is valued so much that the teachers always have a choice of home-made delicacies for morning tea and lunch, and always flowers on the front desk and table, and, most of all, the obvious deep, heartfelt gratitude of parents that their kids are being given such dedicated teaching. 'I was almost ready to give up teaching,' one teacher told me. 'Then I came here.'

Giving thanks, in all its forms, can make the difference between a tired, dispirited teacher and a tired but inspired and dedicated one.

To quote a friend and teacher (and fellow dyslexic) Chris Bedford: 'All children are passionate about something. Identify that something, and find ways of using that passion to reconnect the student to their own learning. No one is "hopeless". They might just be confused or a little lost.'

I have never met a hopeless child or teenager. I have met those who have been ridiculed, humiliated and told that there is no hope for them by their teachers. I have seen them believe it, too.

This is not to say that there are easy solutions. Most aren't. They need hours, months, even years of help, often including help from trained professionals. But 'they are hopeless' is a cop-out. It means, 'We don't even need to try.' Often those who try — or succeed in — helping these kids, face active opposition in schools, because it shows how deeply those responsible have failed. Send the 'hopeless' kids from the classroom, wipe them from your mind. And perhaps — if you are lucky — at 4 am your conscience won't niggle you.

Don't blame teachers for this. As a community we get the education system we are prepared to support, with fundraising, volunteering time and skills, or at the ballot box so a greater proportion of our budget goes to education.

As humans we have no greater responsibility than the care of our children. Nothing — not green sports ovals, not excursions to Canberra — is as important as having every child learn to read, to have access to the education that will most fulfil them all their lives.

Every child. In every school. Or we have failed as human beings.

What our schools could be like

Imagine a school where kids can talk to each other about what they learn, as you do in university tutorials. (As I mentioned before, I only learnt how algebra worked because my friend whispered a clearer explanation than our teacher's.)

Imagine a school where part of every day is spent out of doors, or at least in other parts of the school buildings: practising writing with water pistols in big letters on brick walls; and spending a half-hour quiet session on essay writing under a tree — or even a lesson in that swimming pool, floating on noodles ... And by now most teachers reading this are thinking, Chaos! I'd be hoarse by the first hour just trying to be heard over the noise. Others will be remembering that the ancient Athenian pedagogues were often slaves who had no choice but to pander to the demands of their owners. But there are so many ways we could change the way lessons are given, including ones that don't need much extra money.

The microphone solution

Add a microphone, and noise is no longer a problem. I would love to see every teacher given a small lapel microphone. No raising your voice in class. A whisper could be as effective as a yell. Kids who are easily distracted could be given headphones so all they can hear is the teacher's voice and the lesson. And, yes, they'd often lose the headphones. But at about $3 each a supply isn't going to break the bank, nor at $25 would lapel microphones for teachers, plus a $45 small portable amplifier, the kind I use for workshops here, or Bluetooth connection.

These microphones would also mean that teachers would suffer less voice strain, and the high blood pressure that can come from continually having to raise your voice.

Outdoor classrooms

Kids — and adults — shouldn't sit still at desks for hours each day. It's bad physically; it's bad psychologically. It's also boring and claustrophobic.

Kids need lessons outdoors. Once a teacher has a microphone and a small portable amplifier or Bluetooth connection, kids don't need to be indoors in a quiet environment. Take them outdoors to do something they enjoy: picking vegetables or fruit in the school gardens, a simple, repetitive task that relaxes them and that they enjoy — especially if allowed to eat the strawberries or cherry tomatoes as they pick — and teach them then. Not all lessons can be done without a blackboard, computers or books, but at least one a day can be.

Outdoor classrooms. Laptops are mobile and they have batteries, whiteboards are portable too and wi-fi gives us even more flexibility. Arrange classrooms out of doors, under a tree or under stilt-mounted sub-tropical school buildings.

Add movement

Many kids feel school is a physical prison, stuck as they are behind desks in a room. Some kids only learn easily when moving: see Kinetic learners in Chapter 8. But all kids have energy they need to use or they become restless, especially when they are taken to school by car or bus, and haven't walked or cycled and/or debounced themselves.

About a decade ago I visited a school where I was supposed to talk to about a hundred four- to six-year-olds for two hours. Two hours! I tried to tell them that twenty minutes was about the maximum length of time kids that young can remain focused. The teachers said calmly, 'It will be fine.'

They were right.

We arrived just as school was going in. Instead of a bell there was salsa music. Dancing was compulsory — we danced too (kids can dance in a wheelchair too, though they may need a 'sports' wheelchair to really get into it). Every half an hour throughout my talk the music began again and the kids danced in the classrooms for five minutes. After that, beautifully debounced, they sat and concentrated. As we left, a class of kids had put on wings and were 'flying' around the playground, being butterflies. It was a vision of happiness and beauty I'll keep with me always.

To add movement:

- add music and dance, as above
- add 'moving classrooms'
- create 'new context' classrooms. The most gorgeous library I ever saw had picture-book pages enlarged and Blu-Tacked onto the ceiling. At lunchtime little kids came in and lay on the cushions and read the story as they had their much-needed rest.
- turn every ceiling in the school into a book: picture books for the littlies, limericks and poems for the older kids. Do the same to wall space: turn each into a book, created by the kids, with bright pictures and text.
- make the school grounds 'play friendly' to encourage playing active games, especially imaginative ones. Divide the playground area with low-hedged shrubs, not so high that kids can't be supervised but high enough to create the illusion of 'garden rooms'. Trees give a feeling of privacy without restricting supervision. Kids are much more comfortable if each group feels it has its own space rather than sharing one giant playground.

Let kids talk in class

Every time I give a talk to teachers there are always a few, down the back or along the side, whispering to each other. They probably aren't comparing notes of what they'll have for dinner, but making the noises we humans usually make when we are absorbing information: 'What do you think?', 'Yes, that's exactly right. Remember when …', and so on.

We remember information and absorb techniques best if we can discuss them, comment on them and ask for instructions about them. But when you have twenty-four kids and one teacher, there isn't time for everyone to discuss it with the teacher. So let them talk among themselves.

'But what if they're not talking about the lessons?' I hear you ask. Some of the time they won't be. But as long as mobile phones and other non-lesson distractions aren't allowed, one of the kids chatting will probably be interested enough in the lesson to turn the conversation back to what they are studying. N.B. if most of the class wants to talk about something else, talk to them about it. Can the teaching be made more testing or interesting? Do they simply not want to learn this lesson? If so, do they understand the implications? If you don't get this into your brains now, today or this week, you won't understand the next step, or won't get a good grade? Not all lessons appear relevant at the time (I was twenty-two and working out how much water my homemade tank would hold before I understood the usefulness of geometry). But kids do — mostly — understand the concept of, 'This is/appears to be dumb but we need to do it anyway.'

In the meantime, let them talk, quietly, politely and about what they are studying, and use a microphone and headphones so they don't disrupt other kids who can't learn with noise going on around them. This isn't a licence to have loud exchanges of jokes across the room, to be boorish or to call out insults. Quiet discussion doesn't lead to anarchy.

Make school theirs

Kids spend a large part of their life at school, an environment created and ruled by others. Let them change it.

Australia isn't a loaf of sliced white bread where each slice — or community, family or school — is identical. Some schools have an immense diversity of cultures; others far fewer. Some of these (for instance, schools in remote areas of Australia's north) may be mostly one culture, but one very different from that of southern city kids.

Schools need to reflect the lives of their kids. What would make the connections between your kids, their community and the school stronger and more vital?

There is no one answer to that. Ask! Ask the kids what they'd like and how they'd like to learn. Ask the parents how they would like to be involved. As I write this there is a trial in Arnhem Land in Australia's north of ways to link school with the needs of Indigenous communities.

Three superb schools — all of them state schools — spring to mind when I think of schools that have involved their communities, where, for example, they have adjusted the school year to take into account the peak times for cultural business (making it coincide with school holidays).

The first is a school in a regional area of high unemployment. The principal and teachers decided that every morning assembly would have something to interest the parents as well as the kids, to encourage parents to stay and listen instead of just dropping the kids off. Sometimes it was a music performance by the kids or local choirs, or a talk by a sportsperson.

One such morning's entertainment was a talk from me. As the principal said: 'Once you have parents here, they tend to stay.' That school had the best gardens I've ever seen: dads making sporting areas, a mum and dad in the kitchen teaching kids how to cook and making lunches for that day; parents and grandparents listening to kids reading and helping to spell out the hard words. It was a magic place of love and happiness, not just for the school. The parents might have been officially unemployed, but they knew that the work they were doing was the most valuable of all.

The second school was an outer suburban one, with not more than three children in any class with English as a first language and, I think, thirty-two different 'home' languages spoken by kids at the school. But again, every day that school had an event for parents too — and once again they stayed. Many of them were on temporary protection visas under the terms of which they were not allowed to work.

The third was in far northern Queensland. It was a small, two-teacher school — a husband and wife, possibly sharing a single job (and therefore salary). Older kids helped young ones learn. Lunchtime finished when all the kids had come back from a swim. The day I was there the kids raced out to ask the bus driver if he'd mind waiting for an hour or so, as we were having too much fun to stop. He came in, helped himself to a cuppa and a muffin (made by the kids) and joined in. It was the most flexible school I've ever known. Kids learnt Japanese remotely, via computer lessons, and sold cassowary food trees to Japanese tourists to raise money for the school.

Most Japanese tourists faced with a big-eyed, grinning kid who could speak reasonable Japanese paid well over the dollar they charged per tree, often forking over a twenty-dollar note, which helped pay for instruments for each kid to play in their rock band and orchestra. What they studied every day was agreed upon partly by consensus and partly through guidance from the teachers. But it worked. And their standard of literacy was as high as or higher than that at any school I have ever been to.

Another school I've known allowed kids to bring their dogs and horses to school (agistment paddocks and dogs had a one-week trial period to see if they were 'school trained'). One fabulous school in South Australia had a giant vegie garden, fruit trees and school chooks, and every morning one class got to pick and cook lunch for the rest of the school. The day we were there it was vegetable soup, salad with a dressing invented by the eight-year-old cook, and fruit muffins. Another school in a disadvantaged area of NSW has vegetable gardens maintained by volunteers. All veg can be picked by kids and parents. One of the volunteers says that broccoli is surprisingly popular, as are carrots, potatoes, silverbeet, lettuce and sweet potatoes. Corn and strawberries possibly top the list.

You want to tempt kids to school? Give them food: not just to eat but to pick, grow and take home.

Other ideas for personalising schools include:

- Create murals on school walls. Simple, cheap, quickly and easily painted over, but as soon as kids see the painted wall — or path or school assembly area — they know 'this is ours'.
- Write a serial on the largest wall, a line each day, with each class taking turns to contribute what comes next.
- Create 'graffiti walls' where kids can write or draw, with the only restriction being that it must not hurt anyone else. (Obscenity hurts those who are shocked by it, so it's out too.)
- Give kids garden space: not a garden designed by adults, with kids as slave labour. Ask them what they'd like to grow and make it a joint project.
- Vote each year on whether they want the oval for football, the basketball court for basketball, or could you all change what they're used for? Grazing alpacas?
- But most importantly: *ask*. Every year, ask kids how they'd like to change the school around. Let each class discuss it, decide on what they want, then elect two people from each class to sit on a committee to bring all the ideas together. If it costs money, then help them work out how to raise it. If the school authorities won't agree, sympathise and help work out a compromise. But let kids feel that the place they live in for most of their school years is friendly, and shared by all of them.

Encourage projects

School shouldn't just be a place where kids absorb information. They should also be able to use it, and exchange it, and teach others. Some kids love inventing things. Others like making, repairing, building, growing, nurturing ...

If you have a mob of kids who don't want to come to school, see what they *would* come for. Two of the most effective schemes I've known have been boat building and car repair. In the first, kids with juvenile records worked to build and then sail a boat. In the other, kids were each given a wreck of a car, and volunteer help to turn it into something that could be registered. When they were seventeen, the car was theirs. If they didn't turn up or were in trouble for glue sniffing, theft, etc., they weren't allowed to work on their cars for a certain amount of time.

It worked.

Build a solar car or boat; build a classroom; create a garden; invent an app and sell it for a million dollars (or not): these can be lunchtime and after-school projects, but they can also solve the problem of 'What do we do with our hands while we learn other stuff?'

Have a session each term where kids can talk about what they'd like to invent, either themselves or as group projects, then ask for teacher and community volunteers, through the local paper or TV if necessary, to get them to help make them. No, they may not succeed — or not for a decade or two when they try again at twenty-five. But if Sam's asteroid mining machine works the earth is going to be resource rich when I'm 104. And if he is encouraged to invent now, who knows what he may create as he grows older.

Abandon the paradigm of neat kids sitting quietly with their hands in their laps. That isn't how we humans have learnt for most of our history. It's tidy, and sometimes even a good way to learn. But often it plain doesn't work.

Teach that teachers are human

To many kids, teachers are the enemy: he or she is the one who traps them in a classroom all day, gives them books they are bored with and then makes them do homework. Kids need to be taught that other people — including teachers and parents — have feelings too and especially that they should be thanked for all they do that is beyond their job description. Encourage kids to say, 'Thank you — I enjoyed this afternoon.'

Come to think of it, I don't think I thanked a teacher once all through schooling. It may be a bit late now but: Thank you. You all helped make me who I am today, the good bits, anyway. The other bits are no one's fault but mine.

Lovable libraries for kids

I remember some librarians, in towns and cities, and weep with joy that there are people like them in the world. There was one who did a counselling course because so many people with mental illness, no longer supported by enough health staff, had found the librarian at the desk would listen to the rants that others ran from.

Another, in a library I shall not name, realised that the homeless had found not just a place where they could breathe cool air or warm, but a place to sleep, and dedicated a small room to one side, with bench sofas and an urn with instant coffee, to give them refuge while keeping other clients content.

There is that beautiful school library with enlarged picture books on the ceiling, so small kids can lie on cushions on the floor, and look up and read. There is the National Library, which I know well, and those libraries in other capital cities that not only provide spaces for the cultural events that help create us as a society, but engineer them, inspiring and enabling more books for their collections, more small blocks in the edifice that is the city, our country and our world.

I remember my father's last four years, when the walk to his local library every second day took ten minutes, then forty, then sixty, and then a bus ride. That library was an integral part of the framework of his days, sitting to catch his breath and watch the children at story time, then slowly choosing his next two books, all he could manage with his increasing frailty and walking stick. Where, even in a city of cars and apartments, the librarians knew his name and knew which new books he would like and then, finally, as his memory drifted into the happy parts of his past, gave him books they knew he had read but would have forgotten, and would love all over again.

No matter what form books or their depositories evolve into, it is that compassion, that connection forged between the reader and the book, that creates a library.

You know why we whisper in a library, even though the dragons have left the front desk? Because subconsciously we know that a library is a web of wormholes, matching each reader with each author, linking a billion universes every day. We whisper lest we disturb the power.

KID-FRIENDLY LIBRARIES

Kids are noisier and messier and more active than adults, especially elderly ones like my dad. Which is a good reason to have school libraries and separate areas in a town library for them, not just because that's where the 'suitable for kids' books are.

Just as with classrooms, the perfect library for kids

will be messier and noisier than one for adults. And the books won't last as long.

The following have all been put into practise by superb libraries across Australia.

- Areas where kids and story time can make a noise and not disturb other patrons. Young kids can be a bit frightening to elderly patrons, especially if they grab their walking frames. Other elderly patrons, like my father, will love to watch story time and the kids, so provide chairs for them to enjoy it all too.

- Areas where other patrons can have a cuppa or use computers and not disturb kids or their parents. If the homeless or mentally ill in your neighbourhood see the library as a refuge, entice them to the opposite end of the library with sofas, tea, coffee, biscuits.

- Kid sizes: small chairs, small tables, beanbags, carpeted stairs to sit on with a conversation pit for stories.

- Touchables: kids love to touch books. Have books spread out on the low tables where kids can see them and pick them up, not just formally in shelves or even display shelves. Change the display at least once a week.

- Colours: murals of books and book scenes on the walls; posters, mobiles.

- A picture book blown up to a large size, page by page, on the wall. A new one every month, or week.

- The same on the ceiling, with cushions so little kids can lie back and follow the book as the adult reads it to them. In school libraries, this works well as the last twenty minutes of lunch for kindy kids, so they can have a rest without feeling the pressure of 'a nap'.
- Help: not just someone at the desk to answer questions, but a friendly presence who'll ask, 'Can I help you find what you'd like?'
- Story time every morning at ten.
- An urn and tea and coffee for parents, with a contribution box.
- A 'book of the week' display with snippets of information about it.
- Displays of the kids' books shortlisted by the Children's Book Council of Australia, each state's Premier's awards, Prime Minister's Awards, Indie Awards, and each state's Kids' Choice awards, plus those books to borrow — not just for display.
- Proactive children's librarians who go to schools to tell kids that libraries exist, and are free. (Many — even most — kids don't know this.)
- Pyjama parties once a week at 6 pm, where parents can take kids in their pyjamas for a bedtime story reading.
- Holiday programs.
- Email newsletters (most kids now have an email address) announcing new books, and inviting kids

to submit their own reviews, with links to book blogs for both kids and parents. You may need one for littlies, one for younger readers and another for teenagers. Few teenagers want to read about the latest book for the under-threes.

- A free community room that can also be booked by kids for reading clubs and other societies.
- Computers in the kids' section loaded with kids' games that make early literacy fun.
- A library mascot, preferably large and animal, who the kids can greet by name.
- Friendship. For many kids — and adults — a library is the place where you will always be greeted with a smile, and have your questions answered. Librarians may never know quite how much that is valued.
- Dogs! Many libraries also have reading dogs that *need* to be read to — and the kids love reading to them, too.

It's only paper: encouraging kids to read when they eat (the art of reading with sticky fingers)

Five hundred years ago your books would have been a manuscript, possibly hand-lettered on vellum, the fine skin of young animals like calves or kids, embossed perhaps and maybe even 'illuminated', decorated with rich colours like lapis lazuli and gold leaf. It would have been carefully transcribed by monks or nuns for the love of learning and also to earn funds for their monasteries or convents for staples like dried fish for fast days and winter meals.

Paper is not precious these days. While one could argue that it should be made more expensive in order to conserve trees, it's cheap. And so, really, are paper books. If a book lasts a decade it can be read ten to a thousand times ... even if you have sticky fingers.

When I was a kid you had to have clean hands to read a book. No turning down corners, no scribbling in the margins. Defacing a book was ... well, defacing it: a crime as great as talking in class. A book was sacrosanct and meant to stay pristine till it yellowed naturally and turned brittle.

True book lovers   unless they collect rare and first editions — rarely treat their books with awe. They eat when they read — or rather, most read when they eat. (All meals, even five-star ones, are better with a book at hand.) They read on the beach, while they are sticky with suntan lotion. They drip watermelon and mango juice on the pages, or at least I do.

I reread books often, the first time to see what happens, the second to enjoy the words and the third, fourth and fiftieth times because every time you read a good book you find something new, but also because books can become old friends, good to visit, the equivalent of a cuppa and a hug, which is why I always reread favourites before I go to bed.

Reading those best-loved books is a forensic exercise. Is that brown stain chocolate, gravy or a squished mosquito? Where did the airline boarding-pass bookmark come from, the ferry ticket, the tissue that might have wiped hay fever-y eyes (but of course nothing that might be infectious)?

I love far-from-pristine second-hand books, bought or passed down, ones with comments in the margins or underlinings (Dad was good at that) or just an exclamation mark; I love the books of poetry that always open at the same beloved page.

Which — finally — brings me back to kids and reading. Encourage kids to read at any time, not just with clean chins or fingers. A well-loved book can be a messy one and, anyway, paper soaks up stickiness quite well. Splodges show the new reader that someone has gone this way before, with a sense of happiness and adventure: they're signposts to what's to come. Which reminds me, it's time for an RSI break — a good book. Pass the scones please, darling, and the chilled watermelon. And, in an aside for those who may read the book after I do, those red stains are strawberry jam or watermelon juice, not blood, and a sign that this book has been well loved.

HOW VOLUNTEERS CAN HELP

The evolution of a volunteer tutoring group — Youth Educational Support Service (YESS)

By Angela Marshall

In 2009, a group of Far South Coast residents, who were concerned about poor educational opportunities and outcomes for many local students, met and formed a group that they named the Youth Educational Support Service (YESS). With the support of Narooma High School, the members of YESS were committed to providing one-to-one tutoring, mentoring and support for struggling students. Initially, we focused on trying to improve the retention rates and educational outcomes for Indigenous students in the final years of high school. Very rapidly we realised that most of the problems that 'our' students were struggling with began much earlier in their school lives, involved complex issues of literacy, school attendance and social issues and affected Indigenous and non-Indigenous students in roughly equal numbers.

It was our enormous good fortune that our contact person within the school, the teacher who was at that time in charge of Learning Support, was able to see the enormous potential for the school in having a group of committed volunteers on hand and who also knew a great deal about many of the competing approaches to stubborn literacy problems. What she was able to do was see how these two elements could be harnessed to radically change the lives and educational experiences of the students who had arrived at high school without having been taught to read effectively in primary school — the very students who, without intensive and successful intervention, were most likely to have very poor educational results and become disruptive elements in class detracting from other students' learning experiences.

She suggested that we use a program developed by Macquarie University called the MultiLit (Making Up Lost Time in Literacy) Reading Tutor Program and that we should all be trained in the delivery of this program. That training day was intense and somewhat overwhelming as so much theory and practical tuition had to be absorbed in so little time, but most of the volunteers stuck with it and, once the students were identified and had completed their placement tests, we began tutoring individual Year 7 students one on one in 2010. This commitment to the students and involvement with the school continues today (2014). Once we had a working template for delivering literacy tutoring using trained volunteers we expanded into the feeder primary schools (there will be seven primary schools involved in 2014 as well as Little Yuin Preschool doing pre-literacy work), recruiting and training new volunteers from each community to work in their local schools. YESS operates within the various schools in our area under the direction of the principals and with oversight from the Learning Support staff. YESS has a website which anyone who is interested in developing a volunteer-based tutoring group can access and we can give advice on how we organise our volunteers and deliver the programs — www.yess.org.au.

The organisation of the rosters of volunteers and students, the purchase and allocation of materials, and the provision of a venue as well as the day-to-day administration of the program within the complex machinery of a large high school has been a challenge but one that has been well worth meeting as the results have been so significant. Obviously, it is simpler in the primary schools as the students have much less complicated timetabling and fewer teachers are involved in their daily routines. Each school develops its own routine dictated by the number of trained tutors and struggling readers, available space, and so on.

The two schools with which I have been closely involved over the last five years, Narooma High School and Narooma Public School, are organised so that six students each receive a half-hour session four days a week. Each volunteer is asked to commit to one two-hour session a week. This requires a minimum of eight volunteer tutors although, in practice, the roster requires more than eight volunteers so that if a tutor is ill or goes away for a holiday or has a family crisis or for any number of other reasons there are back-up tutors who can pick up those sessions. It is really important to maintain the intensity of tutoring — there is an enormous drop off in effectiveness if the students miss out on their regular sessions. Five days a week would be ideal but there are practical issues, like sports days and formal assemblies etc., that make this difficult. Also, ten volunteers per school would then be required —

we have found that four days a week is workable and still effective. I would urge any volunteer group contemplating providing reading tutors to a school to be determined not to reduce the frequency to three sessions a week — low-progress readers often have problems with retention of information so the more sessions they receive a week the better the outcomes.

In summary, what we provide is intensive and consistent explicit tuition to each student who has been selected by school staff through testing and ranking against specified criteria. Once a student has been selected for this intervention they receive half an hour of one-to-one tuition four mornings a week by a series of trained volunteer tutors. The three principles — *intensity* (one-to-one, four days a week), *consistency* (trained volunteers delivering a precise and evidence-backed program as it is designed to be delivered) and *explicit instruction* — are the foundation of a successful literacy program.

For a volunteer tutoring program to operate effectively and efficiently within a school it obviously requires:

- good communication with and support from the school.
- one of the volunteer tutors to be prepared to be a coordinator to organise rosters, ensuring that each day there are tutors ready and available to tutor that

day's students; to be the point of communication between the school and the tutors (mainly done by email); and to organise ongoing training of new tutors and refresher courses for existing tutors.

• a system of consistent testing and evaluation to ensure that genuine, ongoing progress is being made.

MultiLit (Making Up Lost Time in Literacy) Reading Tutor Program

The current MultiLit Reading Tutor Program is the result of thirty years of research at Macquarie University into how best to teach students who are struggling to acquire basic literacy skills. The program is not intended for all children, the vast majority of whom will learn to read and write with their peers in the classroom. The basis for the MultiLit Reading Tutor Program is a conviction, backed up by scientifically verified evidence, that effective instruction is the key to learning. The Reading Tutor Program is, as a consequence, continually being evaluated and adjusted to ensure that low-progress readers are instructed and supported in the most effective way possible.

The MultiLit program does not focus on the reasons or underlying causes that are preventing a child from making adequate progress in reading. This approach is called 'non-categorical' and it is used because it has been shown that the different labels have not been found to be particularly useful in determining how a child can best be helped to learn to read. MultiLit has been used with great success in various communities all around Australia and New Zealand in urban, regional and remote areas. It has been used to great effect in communities that have a high number of children from socially or financially disadvantaged backgrounds including with Indigenous communities in Cape York and also with disadvantaged students in Bangalore, India.

To learn to read, low-progress readers require explicit instruction in five areas:

- phonemic awareness — being able to recognise, isolate and manipulate the individual sounds within words
- phonics — the relationship between letters or groups of letters and their sounds
- fluency — reading smoothly and effortlessly, is essential for comprehension and reading enjoyment
- vocabulary knowledge — it is essential that students develop a good and expanding vocabulary
- comprehension — this is what reading is really all about!

The MultiLit mantra is to test before you teach — every session involves testing the students — in an enquiring rather than a judgemental fashion.

Only when a student makes an error do we stop the testing and begin teaching.

It is vitally important that students feel that, although they are being tested, they are not being judged. Encouraging students with ample and completely specific praise throughout the lesson is essential to making the lessons a warm, safe and positive part of a student's day. We want the students to look forward to their sessions and this is only possible if we establish an atmosphere that is light, bright and fun. With every student the tutor can find something to single out and praise — arriving promptly for their lesson, sitting up straight, speaking clearly and audibly, writing with great care ... catch the student being 'good' so that they can be praised and encouraged.

MultiLit is divided into three main elements and approaches the task of learning to read by focusing on the different skill sets required to become an effective reader. Students require intensive, systematic and explicit instruction in all three areas.

WORD ATTACK SKILLS (WAS)

Developing the necessary phonic (word attack) skills is an essential part of any literacy program. These are the skills that allow a student to 'decode' text by using what they have been taught about the associations between sounds and letters or groups of letters. Within WAS there are three main components — accuracy, fluency and spelling (although this is not a spelling program as such).

SIGHT WORDS

By working towards automatic recognition of the 200 MultiLit sight (or high-frequency) words, low-progress readers are able to access a large amount of text. These words are taught as whole words as many of them are phonically irregular and so cannot be decoded but, because they are commonly encountered words, once these have been mastered students can read over half of all texts. These are taught using flashcards that need to be recognised within two seconds.

REINFORCED READING

Using an appropriately challenging book the student is now in a position to apply the skills that they have acquired (in Word Attack Skills and Sight Words) and to read a text to the tutor. It is important that the book is of an appropriate level of difficulty so that they are both challenged (by the occasional new or unfamiliar word) and encouraged (by being able to read over 90% of the text without help). There are three important elements in the MultiLit approach to reading a text:

- Pause
- Prompt
- Praise

PAUSE

When a reader makes an error (either by being unable to read a word or reading it incorrectly) do not jump in immediately to correct them. Either pause for five seconds while they concentrate on the word or (if they have read on) wait until they reach the end of the sentence before stopping them and directing them back to the word that requires 'fixing'. This provides the student with time to self-correct and to apply their knowledge of Word Attack Skills.

PROMPT

If the student does not manage to read the word correctly unaided ask them to look at the word more carefully. Sometimes just being taken back to the beginning of the sentence and rereading it is all that is required. Otherwise, prompt the student to look more carefully at the letters in the word and apply their Word Attack Skills to the word — 'What sound does the first letter make?' or 'What sound do the letters ch together make?' etc. If they are still unable to read the word simply tell them the word, 'The word is chop.' All prompts should be phonic prompts — do not ask them to look at pictures or guess what the word might be ... we want them to look at and read that specific word.

PRAISE

This is a really vital part of the Reinforced Reading phase of the session. You can praise them for reading a word correctly; and when they read a word correctly after you have prompted them; or even for attempting to read a word even if they are not quite successful. You can praise them for reading with expression or for pausing at a full stop or for holding the book neatly and turning the pages without fuss. All praise should be absolutely specific and honest and wholehearted.

Making lessons fun and warm and satisfying is vital to help these low-progress readers to persist in the task of learning to read. These students are often working exceptionally hard at tasks that do not come easily to them so, as a tutor, it is essential to find opportunities throughout the lesson to be positive and encouraging so that their efforts at learning are effective, enjoyable and rewarding.

MultiLit is resource intensive (it requires a large investment in tutors/hours) which is what makes the match between the program and a volunteer organisation such a good fit. Most schools have tight budget constraints and difficult decisions are constantly being made about where their financial and staff resources are allocated — a specialised music program or maybe a theatre production; an elite sports program or a special maths course; excursions for history or science or a debating or chess club. Each and every one of these enriches the students' school and life experiences — and all have to come out of the same pool of money. We have found that by bringing trained volunteers into the schools we can make a real contribution to the individual students with whom we work and support the schools to rise to the challenge of ensuring that every student acquires the literacy skills that are essential to becoming a fully enfranchised member of society.